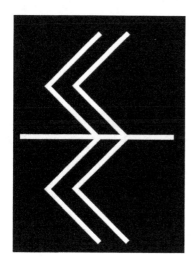

A Broken River Books Original
Broken River Books
Oklahoma City, OK

Copyright 2022 © by David Simmons

Cover art and design by A. A. Medina

Interior design by J David Osborne

All rights reserved.
This is a work of fiction. All names, characters, places, and incidents ware the product of the author's imagination. Where the names of actual celebrities or corporate entities appear, they are used for fictional puposes and do not constitute assertions of fact. Any resemblance to real events or persons, living or dead, is coincidental.

ISBN: 978-1-940885-54-4

Printed in the USA.

GHOSTS OF EAST BALTIMORE

by
David Simmons

BROKEN RIVER BOOKS
OKLAHOMA CITY, OK

In Baltimore, the police have a homicide clearance rate of 34%.
This book is dedicated to the 66%.

*"Coming live from the city Tupac called
the worst city that he's ever been to,
Imagine what I've been through"*
- Mullyman

1

At discharge, the prison provided Worm with a ten dollar bus voucher, which was enough for him to catch the 56 to Sweet Breath's place and cover the trip back to the halfway house before curfew. The correctional officer who processed him handed over his valuables in a freezer bag, smirking as he watched Worm change out of his gray sweatshirt and sweatpants into baggy jeans and an oversized white tee.

Worm dumped out the contents of the bag: three crumpled ten dollar bills, a disposable lighter, loose change and a black, leather Ferragamo belt. At least he had that.

He laced the belt through the loops of his jeans and hitched his pants up. The oversized clothing he wore hung loosely around his wiry frame, his XL white t-shirt a product of a fashion trend gone out of style midway through his bid.

"I see you popped your ID bracelet," said the C.O., pointing at Worm's wrist. "You lucky I don't charge you with destruction of property. I could charge you with that, you know? Send you right back to the pod."

The plastic bracelet had been placed on Worm's left wrist moments after he had been fingerprinted at Central Bookings over two years ago. The bracelets were important, a thing you couldn't lose, and if you did, there would be hell to pay. But it was uncomfortable. And he hated looking at the image of his face staring back at him. The letters of his name, his birthdate. Seeing these things made him physically ill. It would keep him up at night; his own face staring back at him under the muted, yellow glow of the security lighting. The bracelet was supposed to stay on at all times, no matter what, but he had popped the plastic on it, taking it off at night so he could fall asleep and reattaching it with two rubber bands before morning roll call.

"That bracelet is your corrections-issued ID. It's the only way to prove you're you when you leave here. It serves as temporary identification until you get down to the MVA for your permanent shit. That way you don't get locked up for being outside with no identification. You know that's illegal. Loitering."

Worm nodded.

"Your first move needs to be getting down to Bel Air Road for your social security card. Show them folks at the desk your ID bracelet. That's gone help you. Then get your receipt. You gone need to take that receipt down to the MVA for your state-issued ID or driver's license. But you also gone need your birth certificate and two pieces of mail. And don't forget that receipt! And whole time, you still gotta pay the forty or fifty dollars, or whatever that shit is now, to the MVA for your actual state-issued ID. But I'm sure you got all that, right?"

The C.O. was smirking at him again. Worm didn't care. He was free. *Almost.* This is what he had been waiting for. The excitement tickled the inside of his chest like thousands of disembodied centipede legs.

The guard watched him, grinning as he punched in the series of numbers that released the magnetic door lock to the outside world. "See you next time, hear?"

The door slid open and Worm walked into the blinding intensity of natural light. It had been some time since he had felt the warmth of the sun; since he had seen the world illuminated in the clean shine of it. He inhaled through his nose: oil and smoke, the faint ammonia scent of urine in the background. Sawdust soaked in nitroglycerin. The smell of the city.

He blew through twenty dollars copping two balloons from a thin man with nystagmus eyes smoking a Clove in front of the Templo Evangélico Bethel, currently occupied by Narcotics Anonymous for their weekly meeting. The smell of donuts and burnt coffee leaking out an open window made Worm nauseous. He made his way to the bus stop and sat down.

He couldn't say why he bought the dope.

It had been almost two years since he had messed with the shit, staying clean through the majority of his time in prison, working in the optical lab and reading every book in the library. He avoided getting involved in any of the bullshit that comes with confining 2,622 men within a 276,473 square foot space and did his time in his cell, learning lensometry and studying for his ABO certification. He got a job in the prison finishing department, operating the hand wheel.

An older inmate, a nice guy named Qincy who ran the edger, showed him how prescription eyeglass lenses start out as big, thick, hockey puck-looking things called *blanks*.

"It's pronounced *Kinsey*. Like Quincy without the U."

This is how the old man introduced himself.

It never made sense to Worm. In his way of thinking, Quincy without the U would still be pronounced *Quincy*. On account of the way the letter Q worked. An old-timer with kind eyes and a calloused handshake, Quincy without the U showed Worm how to load the blanks—right lens first—into the edger, specify the parameters and start the lens cycle.

When the lenses came out of the machine, the edges were sharp, dangerous if you ran your fingers over them. If somebody got punched in the face with their glasses on, and they had lenses that were fresh out of the edger, and the impact of the punch caused the lens to pop out, and that sharp edged lens went into the person's eye, they would most likely end up blind in that eye.

So Quincy without the U showed him how to put a *safety bevel* on the lenses. That was Worm's job. He would hold the finished lens to the diamond coated wheel at a 45-degree angle, rotating it slowly, thumb over index, index over thumb, smoothing out the sharp edges.

He could get a job doing that, maybe. There was an optical lab in Halethorpe, not too far from the city. He could wake up early, catch a couple buses, make it to the county and back.

In the beginning, at least. In practically no time, he'd be able to get his driver's license renewed, buy a car, drive there. It was a solid plan.

But he needed money now and he couldn't wait the three weeks it would take to get his paperwork submitted, get put on payroll, get his first check. He didn't even have a bank account, so he wouldn't be able to provide a voided check for direct deposit to be set up. No, he needed to link up with Sweet Breath and hit a quick lick. Something quick and easy, not too messy. He just needed some money, just a little bit of bread, enough to afford some new clothes, dress slacks and loafers, something, *anything* to wear to a job interview.

And back to the dope: he didn't have a good answer but he knew that he wanted it. *Needed* it. There were always excuses. He could find blame in the weather. It was a hot, humid day, the oppressive kind of heat that sucks the color out of everything. The high from snorting dope blocked that, made it so you couldn't feel the weather. It could be a hot day or a cold one. After that first hit, that fluffy, cotton ball numbness insulates you and you don't feel shit.

The balloons were fat too. He could feel their weight, rolling them around in his palm like Baoding balls. He decided he would snort one balloon now, save the other for later, so that he could sleep easier at the halfway house.

And that would be it. Just this first night home. He wouldn't get any more. He would go to Halethorpe, get that job. This was a one-time thing. Just to soften the edges. And man, those edges could be sharp sometimes. How the world could just cut into you, slicing off pieces of your body and making you into something colder and harder.

The brakes of the 56 screeching roused Worm from his reverie. He got on the bus and found a seat near the back where he could comfortably nod on the way to Sweet Breath's place. When the doors slammed shut he rolled up his last ten dollar bill, shoved one end in his nose and opened the balloon.

"For just as Jonah was three days and three nights in the belly of the great fish, so will the Son of Man be three days and three nights in the heart of the earth!"

Worm took the bill out of his nose and palmed the balloon. *What type of shit is this?* he thought. A disheveled man standing in the middle of the aisle screamed at the top of his lungs.

"Matthew 12:40! The heart of the earth is hell, ladies and gentlemen." The man waved his arms. Globs of white foam formed in the corners of his mouth. "It's the cosmic darkness. Can you see it?

The other passengers had had enough. "Shut the fuck up!" someone yelled.

"Yeah, stupid!" said a pregnant woman, two children on the seat next to her. "Hey driver. Get him. Ain't nobody tryna hear that shit."

Worm pocketed the balloon and put the bill in his sock. Soon the driver would stop the bus and try to kick the homeless man off. Most likely there would be a struggle and the police would be called. Worm didn't need that kind of negative energy in his life right now. *Save the dope for later.*

"And if your eye causes you to sin, tear it out and throw

it away." The man was grinning now. He held up a pair of needle-nose pliers. "It's better to enter life with one eye than with two eyes and to be thrown into the pits of hell. Matthew 18:9."

Then he jammed the pliers in his eye.

Worm stood up. Some of the passengers that were seated closer to the man started screaming and backing away from the dark tendrils of blood that shot out of his eye socket. The driver slammed on the breaks, bringing the bus to a screeching halt. Vitreous fluid, the color of donut glaze, rolled down the man's cheek.

By the time the driver called 911, Worm had already pushed the back door open and gotten off the bus.

*"Anyone can love a perfect place.
Loving Baltimore takes some resilience."*
- Laura Lippman

2

It was settled. Worm would be walking the rest of the way. Sweet Breath's house was nearby, a twenty-five minute walk at most. He had time before curfew, time to make some moves, stack some paper. *This is just another speed bump on my road to happiness,* Worm thought. Quincy without the U used to say that and Worm had liked the way it sounded. He appropriated the euphemism and looked forward to using it in casual conversation. Hopefully, there would be a chance to drop it and make everyone around him laugh at his cleverness.

The city seemed to pull him forward, like the long fingers of giant phantasms. It was all around him, inside him, wherever he looked. It wasn't that he disliked Baltimore. It was just that he had grown out of it, tired of it. Tired of the city and its ways. Like a relationship gone toxic, they needed time apart. Perhaps they'd see each other again, reunite after a period of time. Or maybe this separation would be a permanent thing. It was scary, the unknown, the idea of leaving the city he had spent his whole life in, but Worm was willing to take that risk.

And no matter how weary of Baltimore he had grown in prison, he knew that he exuded it. The city leaked out of his pores and revealed itself in the way he pronounced his *ou* vowels.

And yet, he was conflicted. It was hard for Worm to ignore the rich history that wafted up from the concrete like heat shimmers as he walked. Being from somewhere mattered. And with the murder rate and bodies being dumped in Leakin Park; BPD with their cold cases and sixteen minute response times; it meant something if you survived Baltimore.

And he had been to other places. The world got funny sometimes.

One time, far out from the city in a place called Westminster, it got a bit funny. On the way out of Baltimore on 795 he saw a sign that said *GOATS*. It didn't say *GOATS FOR SALE* or even the stranger and less likely *GOAT PETTING ZOO*. Just *GOATS*. What did it mean? He would never know and that thought lingered with him, something unanswered that didn't make sense. He swore one day he would drive back to that very spot and draw a question mark after the *S* in the word *GOATS*. That would show them.

He was conflicted. The rest of the world was a strange place, full of absurdities and things that didn't quite jive for Worm. He had seen it on TV and experienced it through the language and behavior of the out-of-towners he had met in prison. People who say "bless your heart" when they really mean "go fuck yourself." Places where you can't pump your own gas. Mixing lemonade and sweet tea and calling it an

Arnold Palmer instead of a Half and Half. Dungeness crabs instead of blue. Signs that say "GOATS" and nothing else. Baltimore was home and home was familiar and he could definitely get that job down in Halethorpe in the optical lab making eyeglasses. Why not?

Do I love it or hate it here? he asked himself. *Do I even know how to leave?*

"Hey Worm."

Simone. It had to be Simone. Worm knew that voice anywhere. How did he not notice her first?

"Hi Simone." He couldn't think of anything clever to say. "It's so good to see you."

She held out her hands, stared at them, concentrating. "Same."

It had been years since he had seen her, smelled her hair or touched her soft skin. What was she doing here? Worm looked down at his loose fitting jeans and baggy white T-shirt. "I ain't even had a shower or been able to cop a new 'fit," he said, grimacing.

"It's fine. You look good."

"Shit, me? Nah, *you* look good. Goddamn, Simone. I really missed you."

Simone kept looking at her hands. When too much awkward silence passed, Worm started talking again.

"You still working at Hopkins?"

Simone looked up at him—hazel eyes with flecks of gold that reminded Worm of the Hubble telescope pictures of nebulas and galaxies that he had seen at the Air and Space museum during a middle school field trip to D.C. "Still at Hopkins."

"Johns Hopkins is the worst, Simone. I don't know why you fuck with them like that."

"Yes, I know."

"They buy up all the houses they can get, leave them vacant for years. All because they want to gentrify everything in the area at the same time. To maximize profits, right? And they can't do that if they don't own all the properties in a neighborhood. So they buy the ones they can, sit on them shits for years while they fall apart, which makes the neighborhood less desirable, then the remaining residents leave and they demolish everything and build a new medical building or more student housing. Plus, even with the incentives they offer for their employees to live in the city, most of them live out in the county anyway and don't pay shit back into the city. They're the biggest landowner in the city and those whores don't even pay property tax."

Simone closed her eyes and sighed. "I know how you feel about Hopkins."

Worm realized he had been ranting. He knew he could be *annoying* when it came to the Hopkins stuff. "I'm sorry. It's all true though."

There was a loud bang, like a wood pallet being dropped on the ground and Worm jumped at the sound of it.

"You good?" Simone asked.

"Yeah. I'm good. I heard you went to the funeral."

"Of course," she said. "I've always been close with your mother. I'm sorry you couldn't be there."

Worm kicked at the ground with one foot. "Yeah. It's messed up. They wouldn't give me a day pass to come see her off. My own mother. Can you believe that shit?"

"I know.. Everyone from the old neighborhood showed up."

"Flag House?"

"Yes. Your mother was loved by so many people."

"Hey, Simone, I've been thinking and—"

"I'm sorry," she said, cutting him off. "I'm sorry I didn't write you back. Everything that went down? It was really hard for me, you know?"

Worm shifted from left foot to right. "You don't need to speak on it. I understand. Outside, life goes on. You have to keep moving."

"Alright." Simone brushed her dreads over her ear, something she did, had always done, something that made Worm's heart feel like a wrecking ball, heavy, crushing ribs and shredding his insides on the way down to his stomach.

"Simone?"

"Yeah?"

"I was thinking. I had a lot of time to think. I've got a power move, something that can get me started. Right now I'm at the halfway house, in the work program. But six months from now, shit will be different. And I was thinking, maybe me and you, maybe we could try—"

"I'm pregnant."

Worm tried to swallow but couldn't. It was like a bran

muffin was lodged in his throat. "Well, that's, that's wonderful for you, Simone. I'm so happy for you."

"Are you?"

Worm let out air. "You always wanted this. You're gonna be an amazing mother, I know it."

"It's really good to see you, Worm." Simone's eyes were wet.

"You too, girl."

Her long, black locs, shiny with oils. Her skin, the color of chestnuts. The gentle curve of her shoulders underneath her teal scrubs.

Worm watched Simone walk away and thought about middle school, holding hands while running out of CVS with stolen packs of Backwoods Sweets and five packs of cheap, translucent, plastic lighters, the ones that came in different colors and how if you removed the metal top and wiggled the notch that controlled the size of the flame, you could make it four or five times the size it usually is, which they referred to as *crack lighters* with their long, big bursts of fire, and how Simone always took the purple ones. He thought about smoking blunts and blowing her shotguns as he wrapped her inside his Eddie Bauer coat, tucked inside, stomachs pressed together like they were sharing a sleeping bag, how their hands explored each other's bodies, nervous and shaking.

Right before she was gone—before she disappeared out of his life again, but this time for good, this time forever—Worm swore that she turned around. Just once. He swore that he caught a glimpse of two swirling pools of gold, tinged by green and coruscating. He was sure that he saw those golden-green eyes make contact with his own and later on he would remember a scenario where she had smiled sadly at him as well.

Why had he started talking shit about Hopkins? What was the point of that? He didn't have to always be the one *right* about things. And things that he was doing nothing to help change or fix.

It had been years since he had seen Simone. Why make their first interaction in so long be a lecture from Professor Worm about *urban renewal* in Baltimore? He figured he had learned how to control himself, spending time in prison, learning how to shut the fuck up.

"Girlfriend! Got that girlfriend!"

Worm's musings were interrupted by the sound of a dopeboy hawking his wares. Worm inhaled sharply. At first, he didn't quite understand what he was seeing. The man wasn't a typical street level dealer, not in the traditional sense at least, and certainly unlike any dopeboy Worm had ever seen before.

Certainly not dressed like *that*.

On the corner of Greenmount and East Chase Street, a man covered head to toe in a shiny, black Zentai suit was shouting. "Got that girlfriend! White girl! Got that boy too! Boyfriend on deck!"

The girlfriend was cocaine and the boyfriend was heroin, that was easy. But the wardrobe choice, well, that didn't seem right. Not at all. Dopeboys in Baltimore were consistent in their attire. White T's, gray joggers, Retro "Cool Grey" Jordan 11's, yellow gold, Cartier Double-C's with the burgundy gradient lenses—this was the dress code, and you didn't really stray too far from it. Black T instead of white. Gold Jesus piece chain but no Cartier glasses. Maybe you'd sub out the Cool Greys for some copper Foamposites, but probably not. And *certainly* not for a black Zentai suit.

Worm had to pass the dopeboy in order to turn right on Chase. He closed his fists and shoved them in his pockets, hitched his pants up. As he passed, the black-clad figure stood silently, his chest pressed out and perfectly still. Worm expected him to shout his advertising slogan as he passed, but no, he just continued to stand there; chest pressed forward, muscles bulging under the black stretch fabric, his arms to his sides with the elbows slightly bent, as if ready to fight. Something about this made Worm get the chills, an icy air that ran over his skin from the back of his neck down to his ankles.

What the fuck? he thought. *Why is he just standing there like that?*

Even with the Zentai suit covering the man's face, Worm felt like he was staring at him. *Through* him. He picked up his pace, bending the corner onto Chase while never taking his eyes off the man.

Worm passed crumbling brick buildings, vacant lots and empty units. The Hi-Mart corner store. A barber shop called Kingdom Cutz. Penn Liquor with the Newport signs and Belvedere Bleu promotional material plastered across the storefront, impossible to see inside. JT Automotive; the 93 Caprice Bubble with the candy apple red, Candy Paint paint job and the police package, sitting out front with the business logo wrapped across the back window. The Recovery Center of Maryland—a pallid-faced man, eyes sunk deep into his aciculate cheekbones, standing out front, smoking a cigarette with shaky hands.

Worm walked and thought about Simone, wondered who the father of her baby was, then wished he hadn't put that thought out into the universe. The last time he had seen her they were at the Cylburn Arboretum, that big botanical garden-type joint over by Cold Spring. They had walked along the path with the neon pink and Actavis-colored azaleas.

"You know these joints are toxic?" he had said. "The honey from the nectar contains this shit called andromedotoxins. They'll fuck you up."

Simone laughed. "Why do you know this?"

"I read it somewhere."

"I like your smile." She ran her finger over his lips, pulling his lower one down a bit.

They sat on a bench under the Japanese maples and Maryland oaks, smoking something special he had picked up from a pop up cannabis event in Georgetown, forty-five miles down south down 95 and the Baltimore Washington Parkway.

"You're the most wildly beautiful woman that I have ever seen," Worm said. "I've always thought that."

Simone smiled. "You've always told me that."

"That's how you know I ain't bluffin."

"It's crazy that we linked back up after all this time."

"Right." Worm nodded and took the joint from her.

The arboretum was a few years ago, which might as well have been forever. He turned left on Homewood Avenue then right on East Biddle Street. There were no conifers or magnolias or stone walking paths here. It was okay to remember nice things, though. Nice things had gotten him through his bid, gotten him through *all* of his bids. Good memories were like precious stones, beautiful, shiny things to be looked upon. It was good to like nice things.

Worm jumped at the belch of a car with a muffler delete. Some kind of Challenger or Hellcat was coming down Biddle Street. All black on black, the same color as death, black rims, five percent tints and the word *Antioch* splattered across the back windshield in red paint. Worm noticed the *T* in the word *Antioch* was in the shape of a cross.

"I do this for the rock boys, who gave me my first pack,
Put it in my hand they knew I was coming back"
- Soduh

3

Worm fondled the balloons in his pocket as he walked and thought about Sweet Breath.

Sweet Breath kept his left foot in a mayonnaise jar of formaldehyde, on top of the safe where he kept his stash. The way the story went, he stopped taking his insulin, started believing he could survive off of sunlight and spirulina alone. That he could somehow *expel* the diabetes from his body with the goodness of a natural lifestyle. Daily Tresiba injections made way for alkaline water baths and colloidal silver smoothies. Not much time passed before he woke up in the hospital with his right foot missing. Upon realizing that he no longer had two feet—which resulted in him breaking the nose of the first nurse he encountered—he was restrained, injected with a sedative and informed that his foot had been amputated due to a necrotizing infection that had gone septic.

A 6 foot 5 inch, 350lbs behemoth with skin the color *and* texture of the meat in a Steak, Egg and Cheese Bagel from

McDonalds. A complete madman. That was his drug dealer origin story, anyway.

The first time Worm had met Sweet Breath he was naked from the waist down, his matted dreadlocks wrapped in a magenta towel that sat atop his head, tall like a church lady's hat.

"I'm airing 'em out," said the fat piece of shit, fanning his genitals with a manilla folder. His veneers—too white and obscenely large for his mouth—sparkled like Chiclets. Swollen fingers glittered silver and turquoise with Navajo jewelry.

"I need a play," Worm had replied. "Whatever you got going on."

Sweet Breath plucked a Flamin' Hot Cheeto from a fold in his scrotum, studied it, flicked it into the darkness of the room. "Say less," he said.

Sweet Breath was a nauseating human being, but thinking back on it, everything went smoothly and he *did* leave with an ounce of fish scale, fronted to him for $1,300 by the same fat piece of shit who made him uncomfortable. But comfort was a luxury that he couldn't afford and it was important that he checked himself anytime he deviated from that way of thinking.

$1,300 an ounce with a street value of eighty dollars per gram (the price would be higher than usual, due to the eighty-pure reading on fishscale) which came out to $2,240. A profit of $940 each time he did the run, and he could do that run two, maybe three times per week, totaling almost $11,280 per month in profits.

And that was *without* cutting. If he cut the shit, those twenty-eight grams of fish could be stretched and chopped, hit with B-12 and mixed with playing cards, shuffled back and forth against the cleanest hard surface he could find until it was closer to thirty-eight grams.

He could easily be bringing home $16,000 per month if he had never gotten locked up, and stayed loyal to the weekly re-up. He needed that same type of hook up right now.

"Oh shit!" someone shouted from across the street. "Look who just came home. If it ain't my man Worm."

Worm watched a man cut across Greenmount Avenue, traffic swerving out of his way as he walked. He was older, wiry—his hair cut short, close to the skull, his waves greased and set. He smiled at Worm with a mouth full of gold teeth.

"Marlon," Worm said. "It's good to see you, man."

"Shit!" Marlon said. "It's all about you right now. You look like they were feeding you good in there. You was hitting those squats and burpies and all that, huh?"

"You already know."

Worm flashed back to his daily routine: 5:00 a.m. wake-up. Wash your face and put your bed down. Get ready for roll call. Back in the cell. 100 star jumps to loosen up. Push-ups next. *Godmakers,* is what they called them. Ten sets of twenty. Each set, a different type: standard, wide, diamond, spartan, incline and pikes.

"You eat anything yet?" Marlon asked.

But Worm didn't hear him. He was doing tricep dips beside his bunk, squeezing his toilet roll for forearm strengthening.

Prisoner squats, lunges, mountain climbers, repeat. One minute planks. Then running in place, shadow boxing, more star jumps. No point in being strong if you couldn't produce the oxygen required to defend yourself.

"My man. You eat since you been home?"

Worm saw Marlon's concerned look, figured he must have drifted off. "My bad. Nah, I haven't. What's good?"

"We gotta get you right then." Marlon raised his hand as if to slap Worm on the back, then hesitated, deciding against it.

Worm looked at the digital clock display above the awning of a liquor store. "I gotta make a move. Maybe if we can make it quick?"

Marlon smiled and shook his head. Two perfectly straight rows of diamond cut, gold fronts sparkled against his mahogany skin. "Just came home and already making moves."

They ate crab cake sandwiches at Mz. Coco's, one of the few businesses still operating in the mostly abandoned Old Town Mall. The outdoor mall had been around for 200 years. All that remained were vacant units and boarded up storefronts. But you could see what it had once been— the rowhouse shops, two-stories with dormers built in the 1820s; 19th century Victorian stores; 20th century Art Deco and Sullivanesque style buildings; stores with cast iron fronts. The hollowed out shells of brick jutted out of the fast food wrappers and broken glass like the fossilized remains of antediluvian beasts.

At one point, the brick pavers of the pedestrian walkway had been lined with planters and glass-globe street lamps and trees that had breathed life into the mall. All that remained now were concrete slabs where the planters once stood and utility hole covers where the lamps were installed. A fountain once served as the focal point, erected in the middle next to a digital clock tower, emblazoned with the words "Old Town Mall." That same fountain now served as a public urinal.

Worm took another bite. The blue crab backfin meat was delicious, though not as good as the jumbo lump his grandmother had used to make her crab cakes. Worm didn't care. He was happy to be eating something he chose to eat, something that wasn't chosen for him. The backfin would do just fine.

"I can pay you back." The crabcake muffled his words.

Marlon waved him off. "Forget about it."

Worm nodded a thank you. "What you doing for work now?"

"I work security. Around the new shopping center they building across from Bay View. It's called Yard 56."

"Near Greektown?"

"Say less. Right on Eastern."

Worm took another bite. "They pay well?"

"Yeah. They alright. Whole time, I might even be able to get you a job, if you interested."

Worm raised an eyebrow. "They hire felons?"

"My bad, champ. You right. I wasn't thinking."

"I ain't mean it like that. I appreciate you thinking of me and even offering."

Marlon wiped his mouth. "What you gone do next?"

"Man. I'm thinking about relocating."

"You bluffin."

"Nah man, listen," Worm continued. "I can do it. I learned how to make eyeglasses and shit when I was in the joint. There's a wholesale lab in Halethorpe, I can get a job there. Stack some bread. Then get the fuck."

Marlon raised his eyebrows. "That's what's up."

"Nah, for real."

They ate the rest of their meal in silence.

Worm looked out the window of Mz. Coco's. At 6:01 p.m on April 4, 1968, Martin Luther King, Jr. was assassinated in Memphis. And in Baltimore, all the knockers in Central district were on duty that day. They were ready for violence, some to prevent it and others to create it. The vacant rowhouse on the corner of Gay and Monument was once a dry cleaner. The windows were broken with bricks and Molotov cocktails. The first fire *officially* reported was at Ideal Furniture Co., now an abandoned building in the 700 block of North Gay Street.

More fires. More explosions.

The knockers sealed off the 400 block of Gay Street, all the way up to the 700 block, the alleys and the side streets, too. Lewis Furniture company was the next one to go up in flames. Two furniture stores, both in the 700 block of Gay Street, both got lit the fuck up.

At 7:00 p.m., two men were burned to death in a fire at Federal and Chester. One of them was black, which was no cause for concern in America. The other man was white, and this meant that the National Guard would deploy 6,000 troops to the city of Baltimore. The governor of Maryland declared a state of emergency. The A&P was looted. More than a dozen stores on Greenmount Avenue burned.

Raging infernos. Fire and brimstone.

People ran through the streets with fruits and vegetables and whole turkeys and garbage pails full of fuel. A row of stores burned to the ground on North Milton while the governor banned the sale of alcohol, firearms and gasoline in Baltimore and all the surrounding counties. A group of opportunists from nearby and affluent Montgomery County fire bombed a jewelry store on North Gay street. When the day ended, there were three dead and seventy injured.

Worm turned towards Marlon. "Whatever happened to that bubble you had?"

"You talkin' bout Lucille?" Marlon shook his head. "Can't believe you remember that joint.

"1996 SS. Dark cherry metallic red. How could I forget?"

"I pre-ordered that bad bitch in late November, 1995. I knew her kind were gonna be extinct soon, so I went all in. I put all my cash on the table with Lucille. I won that hand of car poker."

Worm chuckled. "Car poker."

"Damn right. She was a whale, but she was *my* whale. A killer whale. Lucille spent the winters inside because she wasn't allowed to go out and play in the dirty, salty roads. I had my older brother Micah's joint for that mess. Got his joint when he got killed. Ernestine was her name."

"Ernestine, huh?"

"Ernestine," Marlon nodded, wiping his mouth with a

napkin. "Ernestine was Lucille's winter replacement. She was a high mileage '93 Caprice, white with the police package. She was reliable as a rock until her front seat decided to rot through the floor." Marlon balled up his trash and tossed it in the bin. "Whole time, you get what you pay for."

"Yeah, but what happened to Lucille?"

"You know how it go. Life and shit."

A red CityLink groaned to a halt at the bus stop. The two men watched the flow of people getting on and off the bus.

"Nah man." Worm sucked his teeth. "You loved that car."

Marlon looked away. "You know how it is, how the streets are. One day you the predator, the next you prey. I got old. Sure, I can do security around a high-end, half-built shopping center across town, chasing away scammers and junkies. Shit's different now. These new youngins smell weakness of any kind, they drawn to it, like a moth to a flame."

"Somebody took your shit?"

"Something like that. But not really."

"What's that mean?"

"They *asked* me. But it's not like you got a choice once they come asking."

"They?" Worm asked.

"The Antiochians."

Worm frowned. "Antiochians?"

"Yeah, man."

"What the fuck is an Antiochian?"

"I don't know man, this whole city is weird now."

"What? What the fuck does that mean?"

"I don't know what they are or what they're about. Nobody does. They just showed up here one day. First, over Westside, and now, they're everywhere. I assume they call themselves that because they from Antioch or something."

"Antioch. Like in the Bible?"

"Shit, maybe. Your guess is as good as mine. Maybe Antioch, Illinois or Antioch, California. Lotta places called Antioch."

"The Devil is a liar keep a ratchet for the demons"
 - Smash

4

Sweet Breath opened the door in a fog of Baccarat, his beard braided and perfectly coiffed. Wheelchair bound—by choice, not necessity—he wore his hair high on his head in a beehive, styled in the aesthetic of the Baltimore Hon.

"Ah! Salutations." The fat man's yellowed eyes pooled like egg yolks. "Come in, come in."

Worm followed him into the daylight-style rowhouse, slapping the lintel as he went inside. Through the foyer and passed the kitchen they went, Sweet Breath rolling ahead of him.

"What do you think of Megan Thee Stallion?" he asked, the rolls on the back of his neck dripping sweat. "Do you enjoy her songs? I find her music to be positively titillating."

Worm grunted an affirmation and continued to follow.

"Not only does she promote body positivity, but the woman has turned the misogyny that is ubiquitous in rap music on its head, and furthermore, she has created a path for showcasing female sexuality without it being centered around men. She is an integral part of the rise of intersectional feminism that we see today and I absolutely adore her."

The hallway seemed unnaturally long. Worm had spent his childhood in rowhouses just like this one. They were all the same; similar floor plans and square footage, and the length of this hallway made him uneasy. *How long have I been following him for?* he thought. Eventually they came to a filthy kitchen, illuminated by the unreliable strobe of a faulty parabolic light fixture. Cobwebs hung from the ceiling like party streamers. Worm tried to find somewhere to lean against but the walls and cabinets were all sticky to the touch. He stood in the middle of the kitchen; his hands in his pockets, touching nothing.

Sweet Breath turned the wheelchair around so that he was facing Worm. He was no longer smiling. "You always getting locked up. Somebody put a hex on you?"

Worm laughed. "Nah, man. Just got bad luck is all."

"Bad luck?" Sweet Breath raised a furry eyebrow.

"Yeah. Bad luck. Like, if you threw me into a bathtub full of titties I would probably come out sucking my own dick. That's the type of luck I got."

"This nigga!" bellowed Sweet Breath, slapping his swollen belly and barking out laughter. "A bathtub full of titties, he says!"

"Yeah, man." Worm smiled.

"You ever seen a bathtub full of titties?"

"What? No."

"Shit!" Sweet Breath continued to laugh, his shoulders heaving up and down. He laughed until he coughed, until his coughing turned into uncontrollable hacking. A wad of phlegm the size of a grape hit the wall with a smack. Worm watched the yellow mucus slide down the wall, creeping like it was a living thing.

"So look, right, I was thinking th—"

"Hush now!" The madman smiled, almost apologetically. "I ain't finna front you shit, hear?"

Worm shrugged. "Say less. I ain't got that kind of time anyway."

"Time is a social construct, my boy. Time is merely a psychological property. Space too. All of time and all of space appear simultaneously. Everything that's going to happen has already happened, is happening right now."

"If that were true, then people wouldn't fear death."

Sweet Breath jammed a swollen finger in his nose, twisting it around, scraping the inner walls of his nostril. "Perhaps."

There was a big, gravid pause.

The fat man's eyes lit up like bioluminescent algae. "Do you follow me on Instagram?"

"I don't even have a phone, bro."

"Ha!" Sweet Breath smacked the kitchen counter. Worm watched in slow motion as an empty Red Stripe bottle rolled off the side of the countertop and landed on the floor, shattering. "This motherfucker ain't even got a phone! Type of shit is that?"

"I *literally* just got out today. Less than two hours ago. I ain't even been to my new spot to check in. I came straight to you."

Sweet Breath looked at Worm like a scuff on the toe of a new sneaker. "Motherfucker been home damn near two hours and ain't even got a phone."

"Yeah, but time is a social construct right?"

Sweet Breath whistled. "This nigga think he slick or something."

Worm dialed it back a bit. "I'm just trying to come up, man. I need this work."

"Think he slicker than two electric eels fucking in a bucket of snot."

"It ain't even like that, man."

A lazy siren wailed in the distance. Worm looked at the cracked and warped kitchen counters, the dead flies and brownish-red stains in the sink. A car went by playing club music, the bass thumping rhythmically then fading.

Sweet Breath rolled his wheelchair around the kitchen. "I need a favor and you need money."

Worm nodded.

The fat man stuck his pinky into his nostril and grinded it up there two knuckles deep. He withdrew the swollen digit, studying the ball of dried mucus at the end of it and wiped it off on the side of his wheelchair. "I need you to make a delivery for me. A simple drop off. You walk inside, leave the package, walk out the front. Don't say shit, don't do shit else. That's it."

"Oh ard. How *simple* is simple though?

"Simple enough, yo. Fuck you mean? You ain't gots to collect no money. You droppin' off, not picking up. This shit in and out."

There wasn't much to think about. Money was the reason he had come here. "What's the ticket?"

"Three hundred for an hour of your time. And they'll be more jobs like this one, hear? We about to be tight like two dykes on a dirtbike." Sweet Breath held out car keys and a small, black satchel and smiled and smiled until he was nothing but teeth. "You can take the Lincoln."

"I'mma go harder than Baltimore."

- Jay-Z

5

"Cardiothoracic surgeons are trash," said Alfred. "All of them. I know this nurse, right, and she said she heard a bariatric surgeon talking with a surgical oncologist, right, about how his cardiothoracic surgeon friend can't find work. How yo's been calling all around the Baltimore area, seeing if anybody has a job for him. Plus, she says they're in a turf war with *int rad*."

Sheek unwrapped a wood, dumped the guts in an empty red cup. "What the fuck is *int rad*?"

"Interventional radiology." The bottom corners of Alfred's lips curled downward, wet with smugness.

Sheek rolled his eyes.

"So, what I'm saying is, thoracic surgery is a lot of big time, one time procedures. So they gotta recoup the money with unnecessary shit like endless follow up procedures that nobody really needs."

"Oh, ard."

"So they book you for shit you don't need. Book you and bill you."

Chanel studied her neon green, stiletto nails. *How long does it take to roll up?* she wondered. She snapped gum and blew a bubble.

Alfred coughed up mucus, covering his mouth with the back of his hand. "Did you know there wasn't even a Cold War? Not the way we were told about it. In reality, that shit was just a cover up for two allies—America and Russia—to build super advanced militaries to prepare for an alien invasion. Those nuclear arsenals were never meant for each other. This is still happening. To this day. Look right, North Korea doesn't even exist. Shit not even real. It's just a black site testing ground for Russian-American advanced weapon technology."

"I believe that," said Sheek, breaking down the weed. "Some motherfuckers think that humans lived on Mars, like, we're from there. Originally. Like, Mars is our home but we left it because we fucked up the ecosystem, which is why it ain't got no atmosphere or life now. So the original humans took a ship to escape Mars and crash landed on Earth and that was the meteorite that killed the dinosaurs."

Alfred wiped the back of his hand on the couch. Chanel watched him do it. She looked at Sheek, eyed the blunt. "You almost done with that?" she asked.

Sheek ignored her. "There's a theory that takes it even further. That, like, everything in the Bible that happened before Noah and the flood took place on Mars and Noah's ark was actually a spaceship. The one they took to earth to escape."

"The one that killed the dinosaurs?"

Chanel snorted.

Alfred glared at her. "This guy I know used to volunteer with Make-a-Wish. *Volunteered,* not worked. It's important to make the distinction because the volunteers are the ones who get to do all the fun stuff, like getting the kids amped up about the wish and meeting with their families. They get to be there when the wish is granted. The actual employees on the payroll aren't a part of those things. All of their time is spent on admin bullshit. Endless paperwork and all that."

"Go on," said Sheek.

"So this 16-year-old cancer patient really wanted to meet Wiz Khalifa. He was scheduled for a bone marrow transplant and they wanted to get his wish out of the way first. So Wiz showed up and spent the day with the kid and his family. They talked and chilled and at some point Wiz Khalifa and the kid went for a walk. When they came back from the walk, yo was higher than giraffe pussy. That was a great day for the kid and his family. He died five weeks later. The kid, not Wiz Khalifa."

"OK, but how is that a conspiracy?" asked Chanel. "That just sounds like Wiz Khalifa being cool."

"Right," Alfred said, rolling his eyes. "Everything was all good at first. Except for the fact that Wiz Khalifa was on tour in Europe at the time, so there's no way it could have been Wiz Khalifa. See what I'm saying?"

"So they used a Wiz Khalifa impersonator?"

Alfred shook his head.

"No," Sheek groaned. "You don't get it. He's saying they used a clone. Celebrities are always being cloned. They fucked up with this one though. They really pulled back the curtain this time."

Chanel burst out laughing. Her gold hoop earrings jiggled and caught the light. "You gotta be kidding me."

"There's nothing funny about that," said Alfred. "He's giving you gems. These are facts."

"How about the United States government importing cocaine to fund pro American rebels in Central America during the '80s?" asked Chanel. "And let's not forget how that led to the crack epidemic which had the sole purpose of ruining black generational wealth."

"That's not a conspiracy," said Sheek, twisting the blunt and sealing it with spit. "Everyone knows that shit happened. Not a conspiracy if everyone knows it."

Chanel shrugged and fingered the gold name necklace that rested below her throat. "It was a conspiracy back when it was happening."

Sheek sparked the blunt. Finally. Chanel watched him bring it to his crusty lips.

"Nestle sends representatives to South American hospitals dressed in nurse outfits to make women feel like bad mothers if they don't give their babies formula instead of breast milk," said Sheek, passing the blunt to Alfred. "Then they buy the land rights to the areas where the water supply is so they can produce their shit, but also so the new mothers don't have access to clean water for free anymore, so they can't make formula and they no longer produce breastmilk cause they dependent on the formula so all their fucking babies die."

Alfred hit the J. "Not a conspiracy if it's true."

The weed finally made its way around to Chanel. She put

it to her lips and pulled, doing her best not to coat the mouth end with her lip gloss.

"Y'all tryna get *high* high, or nah?" Alfred dumped a pill bottle onto the coffee table. Three, blue, 30mg M-Boxes hit the glass. "These joints are better than the A-215's."

Chanel shrugged. "They look like regular M-Boxes."

"Yeah, but Sweet Breath said they pressed. Homemade."

"How are pressed joints ever better?" Chanel asked.

"He said it's like, the old school Opana joints or some shit. Same chemicals."

"Oxymorphone?" asked Chanel, the back of her neck tingling. "They stopped making Opana a long time ago."

"Man, I don't give a fuck," Sheek said. "Bust me down."

Alfred laid a dollar bill over the pills and pressed the edges down. He turned a Bic lighter on its side and rubbed it up and down the length of the bill, crushing the pills underneath. "Let's get it."

"I'm ready," said Chanel.

Alfred used a razor blade to scrape the Oxy powder off the dollar bill, adding it to the small, blue pile on the coffee table. He put the bill in his nose and ducked down into the powder. "Goddamn," he said, lifting his head up, wiping his nose. "Here."

Sheek took the bill from Alfred and dipped it in the pile. He snorted his shit and sat on the hardwood floor cross legged. Chanel was last, and for last, she didn't make out too bad. They had left her a full pill, at least. She used her own bill, a twenty she pulled out of her sock and rolled up into a tight tube.

She felt the burn in her sinuses; the sweet, blue candy-flavored drip in her throat. Billions of neurons like tree roots, absorbing messages like water and nutrients. She could feel each neuron. She could feel the neurotransmitters inside every neuron in her brain and spinal cord being received by the dendrites, passing the nucleus, and into the axon. She could feel the sodium and potassium trade places and then switch back to their original positions. Chemical smells filled the air. She ran her tongue along the back of her teeth and tasted metal.

Across the room from her, at a distance that seemed impossibly far, Alfred melted. His clothing attached itself to the cushions, his jeans to the fabric of the couch. It was impossible to tell where Alfred ended and couch began.

What a strange thought? Sledgehammers pounded wet sand inside of Chanel's head. *Is that thought my own? And if not, to whom would it belong?*

A hole tore open in the ceiling. Chanel looked up and saw the night sky; a menacing, Stygian vortex that churned. Debris fell around her, splintering furniture and crushing the detritus strewn about the room. None of the falling drywall touched her, as if she had a protective ring around her. A ceiling joist above the couch snapped, then hung at an angle. She watched it dangle precariously, then fall down, the pointed end impaling Alfred through his throat. She tried to get out of her seat but could not.

Her body had become part of the folding chair she was sitting in. She rubbed her arm, then rubbed the metal of the chair. Dread soaked her down. She was unsure which was flesh and which was metal. Her tactile response lied to her. She could not trust it.

How is this happening? she thought. *What's happening to me?*

Electricity sparked and crackled behind her wisdom teeth. But that simply couldn't be. She no longer had her wisdom teeth. They had been removed when she was fourteen, three of them impacted. But she could feel them, thick and slippery in the back of her mouth, the molars rising out of her gums. An itchiness. She explored her mouth with her tongue, flicked it against the backs of her teeth. And yet, she had the memory of the oral surgeon's office, the mustard walls and popcorn ceiling. She had used her imagination to create images in the vermiculite stipple. She remembered everything.

Is that memory even mine? she wondered.

"What's that?"

It was Alfred.

But he was dead. She had just watched him die. And yet, she watched him now—his gaping mouth open to the black sky that leaked through the hole in the ceiling, his head pushed back at an impossible angle. Had he heard her thoughts, or had she spoken out loud? How was Alfred speaking if he was dead? Were her thoughts out loud, and furthermore, were they even her own? Something was pushing through her, filling her with its mass.

"What did you assholes put in this shit?"

She didn't know if she had actually spoken. The words came out of her mouth, passed over her lips, and yet, her teeth had remained clenched together. The taste of blood, like wet nickels, permeated.

"It's the cosmic darkness," Alfred said, speaking from the hole in his throat. "Can you see it?"

She came unglued from the folding chair. Her body vibrated forward, her front teeth leading her onward. She removed her leggings, peeling them from her body like a snake shedding its skin. The house shook, cracks forming in the drywall. She stood on the couch, planting a leg on each side of Alfred, straddling him. Another ceiling joist collapsed. Chanel lowered her body, sliding herself into the opening in Alfred's throat. She rode him, rubbing herself against the split open neck. Blood ran down her legs, a pool of it growing between her toned thighs. Saliva clicked in her throat.

She threw her head back and howled. Above her, the sky was a bloody mouth the color of balsamic vinegar. She ground her sex down, harder and faster, until Alfred's head came off. Angry, red ribbons kept the head attached to the neck, so that it didn't come apart completely and tumble down the back of the couch. Chanel continued to gyrate atop the exposed trachea, using her hands to pack the torn thyroid cartilage deeper inside her.

Sheek lay trapped under the debris, his heart throbbing in his chest. The skin of his neck felt thin and membranous; the back of his exposed forearm a translucent blue.

"Where is it?" he asked, his voice rising in panic. "Where is it? My chitinous integument? Where did it go?"

Chanel cocked her head to the side, ear up, listening. The room smelled of copper and plaster. There was a wet snap and the remaining flesh that held Alfred's neck together gave up. The head tumbled behind the couch and lay there, face up, the mouth stretched wide.

"Has anyone seen my chitinous integument?" Sheek pleaded, tears running down his cheeks. "Please? Is there anybody out there?"

Chanel jumped off the couch and landed on all fours. She crawled towards Sheek. The hole in the ceiling moved like black water circling a sink drain.

"My integument," he cried. "I'm too exposed without it. Without my chitinous integument, I'm too exposed. Without my exoskeleton, it's all flesh. Weak, soft flesh."

Chanel did not hear this. Instead, she remembered being in elementary school in Mr. Kinja's class, sitting towards the back, at her desk in the fourth row, her loose leaf binder the color of grape soda. Intricate designs and geometric patterns flowed across the front of the binder. She had learned that if you pressed down on the plastic sleeve while drawing your lines, the plastic would pop up from the surface, creating an embossed look. Then it was her name being called on the intercom, telling her to come to the principal's office. She ran her fingers across the raised surface of her binder and cried softly.

The classroom flickered and she was back in the living room. Alfred's head moaned from behind the couch. The sky roared above.

"Silence is golden," said Alfred's head. "But so is piss if you don't drink enough water."

The room began to undulate like ocean waters beneath a glass bottom catamaran and Chanel was back in third grade, in the principal's office, telling him how Zion Mosley had strangled her while two of the other boys—Kim and Kenny—had stood on each side of her, pulling apart her knees and spreading her legs open.

"Now Chanel," said the principal, "are you absolutely sure?"

Chanel was sure. She was sure that Zion pulled up her dress, his uncut nails cutting into the skin of her stomach as he pulled it up to her neck.

"When we tell lies, we hurt everyone. Are you sure that what you say happened *actually* happened?"

It was Alfred's disembodied head talking to her. The head was propped up on the principal's desk in a pool of blood. She traced the embossed cover of her loose leaf binder and her bladder released. She urinated freely, the warmth of it bringing her back to the living room.

Sheek could not determine if he was alive or *not* alive. He knew he was not dead, although being without his chitinous integument for so long made him wish he were. The soft, diaphanous carapace that sheathed him provided no warmth or shelter, no sense of security. He lay prostrate on the hardwood floor, his body sucking up the convection currents that flowed through the mantle of the earth. Tectonic plates shifted at an almost imperceptible pace. They moved under his ribcage, returning to the mantle.

Subduction.

Collision.

Sheek turned over so that he was on his stomach. He dragged himself forward, slaistering through the chunks of drywall and broken furniture. The loneliness of being without his integument was overwhelming. He remained on his belly, using his arms to gather debris, bringing the wreckage towards his chest and sweeping it up over his head and onto his back, burying himself in the destruction of the living room.

"It's no chitinous integument," he said. "But it will have to do."

Chanel became aware of herself. For a moment she understood what was happening. The drugs had been laced. The drugs she had taken had been touched with something new, something dangerous and destructive, something that brought out the violent carnality in a person and—

That didn't explain the hole in the ceiling; the giant, virulent portal to another dimension that whirled above her. A drug could not do these things, which meant that all of this was real, that these were not hallucinations and—

The effect was galvanic. Chanel's body began to seize with awareness. The veil had been torn from top to bottom. God would never again dwell in a place of such weakness, so little endurance. She would need a new skin. Flesh and blood and bone were de rigueur. The shedding of blood and the reinvention of her flesh would bring God back to the world. This was a hungry God, a carnivorous God, one that came from a place of sweat and hunger, a hot, mucilaginous place, a place of voracity and want.

She found Sheek under piles of broken furniture and

pizza boxes and MD 20/20 bottles and chunks of drywall. She brushed away the wreckage and mounted his back.

"Oh hello!" he yelped. "Did you find it? Did you find my chitinous integument? If you simply give it back to me I would be forever grateful."

Chanel used her arms to hold Sheek down. She brought her face close to his back and tore out a mouthful of flesh. She went up his shoulder blades, gorging herself on his meat, sucking him into her mouth, pulling with her teeth, devouring more of him. She used her hands to spread the skin of his neck open, tearing out pieces of muscle with her teeth.

Sheek did not cry out in pain. He did not wince or flinch or shrink away at Chanel's gnawing. He spoke softly, carefully enunciating his words like a child as tears flowed freely. "Something isn't right. Oh no. No, not at all."

Chanel looked around her and was once again reeled back to reality. She lay upon the body of what was once the junky named Sheek. She pressed her cheek to his back. *This is all a bad trip*, she told herself. *I'm going to sober up eventually and then all this shit will go away.* And yet, Alfred's viscera still radiated heat inside of her. His blood coagulated between her thighs. These sensations were not imagined. Above her, a storm raged. She leaned back and bared her teeth at the unearthly, black ebullition in the ceiling of the rowhouse that bloomed like blood in a syringe. She tried to scream but her voice caught in her throat.

Chanel pressed her thumbs into the corners of her eyes and pulled.

*"It's like I turnt up when I fell back,
I put sixes all in some gel caps"*
- YG Teck

6

Worm found the Lincoln Mark VIII parked in the alley behind the rowhouse. A broken, orange sewer pipe coughed up piss and shit into the ragweed and garlic mustard that grew from the cracks in the pavement. Worm identified the broken sewer pipe as being made of Orangeburg, due to the color.

Orangeburg.

Another reason to hate Baltimore.

Goddamn, he was so conflicted.

Bituminized fiber pipe that should have been replaced with PVC and ABS ages ago. Wood pulp, sealed with liquified coal tar pitch as a cheap alternative to metal conduit. That shit fell apart in less than ten years. Building codes would never include Orangeburg on their acceptable materials list, and they hadn't for some time, and yet, there it was: a broken, Orangeburg sewer pipe, vomiting feces and urine all over the city. Worm wondered if anyone had called the authorities about it, and then felt stupid for thinking that a phone call would have made a difference. The public works department wasn't going to do anything about it.

He put the keys in the ignition of the Mark VIII and turned the engine over, which stalled for a bit before coming to life. He made a right onto Ensor, then an immediate right on East Biddle Street. He cruised through Holbrook, where a chiseled, dark skinned man did push-ups in the middle of the sidewalk, and made a slight left on Harford Avenue. The blue brick building that used to house Bidford's Deli shrunk in his rear view.

Baltimore was a city built on enforced segregation and restrictive housing covenants. East Biddle Street used to be Biddle Alley which used to be called "Lung Alley" due to all the cholera, typhoid and tuberculosis outbreaks. It was where they sent the black population to keep them far away from the more desirable Eutaw Place. 100 years ago, the law said that *no Negro could move into a block in which more than half the residents were white and that no white could move into a block that was more than half black.* You couldn't develop a street in Baltimore city without first declaring whether it was for white or black folks.

He could hear Mr. Draghoun speaking through him. It was crazy. That man had made quite an impression on him. When there was nowhere to go after school, nowhere warm at least, he could count on Mr. Draghoun for a Surge from the cafeteria vending machine he never had money for.

"The racism here is built into the architecture of the city," he would say. "It isn't just an outward thing, which it is, but it's built into the urban planning and the way the roads work, how they destroyed things on purpose. How they ran a highway to nowhere right through a beautiful neighborhood, Harlem Park, right?"

Worm thought about that shit all the time, how nefarious it was.

He passed three blocks of crumbling, faded, red brick, Italianate-style houses with arched entryways, all of them boarded up and covered in graffiti. One of the buildings was missing its roof and most of its third floor, as if a Kaiju had taken a huge chomp out of the bracketed cornice. Worm wondered what it looked like inside, what animals might be nesting there.

The historically black Westside was worse, as far as the architecture. Unlike the contiguous neighborhoods of the Eastside, the windy roads, unusual carve outs and undeveloped land made it so nobody had a reason for crossing streets like Martin Luther King Boulevard. The lack of commercial development and pedestrian crossings meant there was no push to go to either side, especially the black side.

It was built into the architecture.

It's the cosmic darkness. Can you see it?

Worm always felt that the city was haunted. So many abandoned rowhouses and vacant buildings. 15,000 as far as the last estimate he had heard on the prison television. That's a lot of abandoned buildings with sad memories and dark energy. Angry ghosts and vengeful spirits.

If you believe in that shit.

"The green spaces over West are few and far between. There's nothing like Patterson Park—its tennis courts and skate parks—or any of the other idyllic slivers of nature that you can find on the Eastside. And Patterson Park? That place was built on top of hate. There have been Klu Klux Klan rallies there as recently as 1970."

That was Worm's 9th grade social studies, or history teacher, or whatever it was called all the way back in the fucking '90s.

Mr. Draghoun.

A stand up guy right there.

He had talked about these things in class instead of sticking to the curriculum. Worm had been interested in ways he hadn't been with other subjects in school. Something about this seemed more necessary, more in need of something immediate to happen. Someone needed to take action, make changes.

"33rd and Greenmount is the Great Wall in Baltimore. The Iron Curtain, if you will." Mr. Draghoun would chuckle in a sad way, maybe an exhausted way, waggling his bushy eyebrows up and down like woolly bear caterpillars crawling across his face. "The newspapers played a critical role in the segregation that plagued the city. Up until 1969, the Baltimore Sun still listed properties according to race, a full year *after* the Fair Housing Act was passed. Would you believe it?"

Worm got stuck at the light on Federal Street and played with the stereo. Bass throbbed from a black Acura in the lane to the right of him. The light turned green and he pulled off, tires squealing. The yellow and red signage of Torino's Carry

Out streaked by on his left. He went further up Harford Avenue until it turned into Harford Road, the industrial gray sky of the Eastside fading in the rear view mirror as he left the city. Project highrises made way for lower architecture. Worm looked out the window as he passed brick rowhouses and liquor stores, pastel neon lettering and going-out-of-business signs in front of businesses that never went out of business.

This was Parkville.

This was a place where white people ran away to during the *white flight* period after the riots. It was new and it was decent. Little red brick single family homes with chain link fences. Rowhouses and nicely manicured lawns.

And then the opiate epidemic ruined *all* of that.

Now it was just…gross. Suboxone wrappers all over the sidewalk. Broken glass and clusters of trash rolling through the street like tumbleweeds in a western flick. Just worn down in general, like most of white america that had been fucked up by Oxy and fentanyl and heroin.

Driving through there, it always looked so gray. It was like a daguerreotype, that early way of taking pictures, flashes of faces on a silver reflective surface.

Worm looked in his phone for the address Sweet Breath had given him. *3301 Woodholme.* He cruised down Hartford until he saw Woodholme, turned left and then pulled up slowly in front of a red brick rowhouse with a tiny plot of yellow grass and dead leaves that served as a front yard. A turned over tricycle jutted out of the dried foliage like a red tongue.

3301.

This was the one.

Worm put the car in park and killed the ignition. The lights were off inside the house but a few late model cars were parked against the curb. He got out of the car and walked up the steps. When he knocked, the door creaked open. The smell that came out hit Worm in his face like a smack. It was state fair vomit after eating too much cotton candy—sickly, sweet rot. Dried syrup. Sweet plums that had gone bad.

A few years back, Worm had taken an exit ramp off the Beltway where a deer had laid down across the road, making swerving out of the way impossible without slamming into the barrier walls, so he had no choice but to drive directly over it. He hit it with a loud thump, kept on going. For weeks after, everytime he started the engine, the smell of cooking meat would rise into the air. Worm could tell it was coming from the undercarriage. No matter how many times he washed that ride, it always smelled like rotting ground beef.

That same sweet smell came out of the house now.

Fuck this, Worm thought, and started to turn back to the car. He made it a few steps before something solid hit him in the back of the head, causing his vision to burst into the color of a cracked iPhone screen before blinking out completely.

*"Fuck sitting in a cell with a pillow beside you,
It's a free ride to hell and I'm willing to drive you"*
- Getum Verb

7

Worm dreamed he was back in the holding cell at D.O.C., waiting for the van to arrive so it could take him to prison. Once he made it inside they would get him state greens and fresh socks, flip flops and the like. More than anything, he wanted to get out of the clothes he was wearing. The knockers had roughed him up a bit on the way to Eager Street and the blood in his hair had congealed.

"It don't matter what those papers say," said the intake officer. "I can't put you in Gen Pop if you don't get your shots."

"Nah, I'm saying though," Worm tried to reply, "it's just the TB shot I can't get. You see, when I was a kid I was exposed to—"

The guard wiped his nose with a hand the size of a baseball mitt. "Fuck all that. You gotta go to medical and medical gotta give you that shot. Like I said, I can't put you in Gen Pop if you ain't got your shots, and I gotta put you in Gen Pop."

"But it's just the TB shot I can't get," said Worm, holding out his note from the doctor, the one he had paid his lawyer an extra five hundred dollars to have notarized and submitted to the judge before his transfer to state prison went in. "I can get all the others. The blood test, whatever, it's nothing."

"Let me level with you, because you seem like a nice guy. Now if you weren't a nice guy, I would just fuck your face up a bit and charge you with Maryland codes 3-201 and 3-203. That shit there? That's assault on a correctional officer. It's a misdemeanor without injury, sure, but you can get another ten years added on to your bid because you're already locked up."

Worm grimaced.

"Now since you're a nice guy," the intake officer continued, "this is what I'm going to do. I'm finna' give you some options. If you don't want to get the shots, I can throw you in the hole for a couple of days, let you ruminate a bit. If you still don't wanna get the shots after that, I can fuck your face up a little and charge you with Maryland codes 3-201 and 3-203. Need I remind you what those are again?"

Worm shook his head.

"You in here for drug shit? I hope you ain't in here for drug shit."

"Not my thing," Worm lied.

"Lemme tell you something about drugs. I know all about addiction, my boy. I used to have a problem with red hot chili peppers."

Worm raised an eyebrow. "The band?"

"No motherfucker! The actual peppers. Don't nobody care about no under the fucking bridge. Damn. I'm talkin 'bout peppers. Jalapenos, cayenne, habaneros, all that there. All that capsaicin gets you lit up. Endorphins buzzing."

"Oh ard."

The intake officer led him down the hall and punched a series of numbers into a keypad. The door swung open with a click, followed by a low buzzing noise. "Your tolerance goes up and you figure, 'well, guess I'll just use more hot sauce.' Next thing you know, you're cuttin' your shit with Scotch bonnets and Carolina Reapers, trying anything to get that next high. It works for a while but eventually you wind up with your tastebuds having cravings your stomach lining can't rock with."

"It's a slippery slope," Worm said.

The intake officer pushed Worm ahead and kept talking. "I've backed off that nonsense, tapered myself off until I got that shit under control. Nowadays I only do it on special occasions and the salsa at my favorite Mexican joint tastes spicy again! Don't go chasing that endorphin buzz, it's no good for you."

Later on, when Worm was in his cell with a firm, red lump the size of a golf ball rising from his forearm, he sulked in a grey fog of loneliness. His cell buddy was less than four feet away from him, and yet, it was like he was the only one in that six by nine fish tank.

"It be the niggas out here puttin in work that be rattin and shit, yo. The certified ones. That's what got me fucked up. How can you put in work and then get jammed up for something you did and then tell on the next man, yo?"

His cell buddy was talking to him.

"That shit crazy. That's a dangerous nigga. A nigga that'll snitch on you *and* kill you. You don't even, you don't even really wanna, knamean, you don't even really wanna fuck with a nigga because you know if you don't kill him he'll fuck around and kill you, but if you do go at him and you don't get him, he gone tell on you! So you, like, in a no win situation with shit like that, you feel me?"

"Ok," Worm said.

"They had me over there, yo. I was over Steel Side, two years, twenty-two and two, you know what it is. Facing triple life twenty-five. Shorty ain't never coming home. This, this, that and the third. Came home for like nine months, coolin. And now I'm back in on some VOP shit. You know."

Worm picked at the tuberculin skin test welt that burned hot on his arm. "That's what's up."

*"Junkies walkin round the block I got em lined up on the wall,
Them dope crowds look like after school at Mondawmin Mall"*

- Lor Scoota

8

When Worm came to, he was zip tied to a radiator, his back against the wall and his legs spread out in front of him. It felt like a million ball bearings bounced around the inside of his skull, ricocheting against the bone. He pulled at the plastic that bound his right wrist. It was secure. He pulled harder and the radiator moved. Perhaps it could be ripped off the wall if one were to use enough force.

He took in his surroundings. His left arm was still free. He rummaged through his pockets, found the car keys. The floor he sat on was concrete, damp with dark spots that looked like oil stains. He no longer had the black satchel that Sweet Breath had given him. A single, bare lightbulb hung from the ceiling by a frayed piece of flex, bathing the room in a phosphorescent glow. No windows. The faint smell of charcoal and ammonia. An ancient refrigerator humming in the corner of the room. The walls were red brick, illuminated by the faint glow of the single bulb—the same red brick of the rowhouse on Woodholme.

Instantly, Worm remembered where he was, what had happened. He was in Parkville. For the purpose of making money. To drop a package off for Sweet Breath. This was his first day out. He was Mr. Just Came Home. He only had until 9:00 p.m. to make it back to the halfway house. Someone had knocked him out on the front porch. He touched the back of his head, rubbed his wet fingers together. *Blood.*

Worm heard a door open somewhere above him. After a few moments of silence he heard footsteps coming down the stairs. *Wet* footsteps, suction sounds, like walking in mud.

By the time Worm could see its face, it had lowered itself to the ground and was crawling on all fours. It seemed to be human—perhaps it *had been* at some point—but it had no discernible facial features beyond a jagged gash in the lower part of its face where a mouth should be. The smell of decaying meat hung thick in the air.

Worm tried to swing on the creature with his left fist but it ducked out of the way and buried its head in his lap. He felt a part of himself pull away, tear off and then separate. Then, fire. When the creature pulled away from Worm's lap it came away with a piece of his thigh. Tears welled up in his eyes. Through the wetness, he saw a blurry image of the creature choking down his flesh, throwing its head back and hacking, like it was having trouble getting it down. It spit out a piece of blue jeans. Worm threw up all over himself and passed out again.

"I got my coke connect from out my father's phone"
 - Getum Verb

9

His earliest memory was of caramel, not of *actual* caramel, but of an imagined caramel that materialized out of thin air and hovered above his father's head. The kitchen of their Flag House Courts sixth floor apartment smelled like rat shit and water damage. A wood-tip Black and Mild smoldered in a coffee mug. Worm flicked the light switch and watched the roaches scatter, some of them big enough for him to hear the sound of their thorax rubbing against the linoleum countertops.

"This shit is in your blood." Worm's father leaned against the stove. He wore a crisp, white v-neck tucked into burgundy, rayon slacks. Water boiled in a large pot behind him.

"You can't let it bubble too long," he said, gathering his long, black hair into a ponytail, pulling it back tight and high on his head. "Lettin' it cook too long, that's how you fuck it up. If you burn it, you can't just start over and try again, feel me? If you burn it, it's all bad. You understand?"

Worm nodded.

His father's name was Ray and Ray was the unblinking, all-powerful ruler of their small apartment. His word was law. God was made in his image. Ray took a ziplock bag out of his back pocket and put it on the counter next to an orange box of Arm & Hammer. He opened the top cabinet and came back with a Pyrex measuring cup.

"This shit here is from 1997," he said, holding out the Pyrex. "That's important. World Kitchen bought Pyrex in 1998, then switched up the formula, making these joints less resistant to temperature changes and more likely to break on you. This one's from before they switched up the formula"

3-6 Mafia played on the Aiwa stereo. The Roland 808 hi-hats and bass drops droned on at seventy-two beats per minute.

"Pay attention now. Four parts to one part baking soda. Too much cut, that's another way to burn your shit. We gone start with four grams. So, how much cut we need?"

"One gram," Worm replied.

"That's right. Good."

Ray put a red, solo cup on top of the digital scale and mashed the *tare* button back to zero. He emptied the ziplock bag into the cup until the LED display read *4.00*, then poured the contents of the cup into the Pyrex. He did the same thing with the baking soda, but stopped when the display on the scale hit *1.00*. Stray droplets went over the edge of the pot and dripped back onto the flame with a hiss. Ray used a syringe to measure out 50ml of bottled water into the Pyrex. He mixed it all up with a butter knife, whipping it around the bottom of the measuring cup until it turned into paste.

"Water soluble. What that mean?"

"It dissolves in water," said Worm.

"Right." Ray put the Pyrex in the pot of boiling water. "Cocaine is a salt. Salts have high solubility but no volatility. You can't smoke powder cocaine. So if you try to smoke it before you whip it up, it's just gone get hotter and hotter until you destroy it. You cook that shit up? Well, now you can smoke it. And what that mean?"

"Higher bioavailability?"

"Boy, don't answer no question with a question in your voice."

Worm nodded.

"So, yeah, bioavailability. The membranes in your nasal passages got some surface area, sure. Not like the lungs, though. Lungs got between 500 and 700 square feet to work with. That's bigger than this apartment. More surface area means faster absorption. Faster absorption means you getting higher faster, and way harder. But that also means it wears off faster. So they gotta come back for more, way more often than if they was just snorting regular powder. That's pure capitalism, boy. Low opportunity cost for the distributor. Market prices based entirely on taking profits. Weakness and inefficiency can't survive in that kind of environment. The market snuffs 'em out."

The cocaine-baking soda-water amalgam gently simmered, tiny white bubbles breaking the surface like foamy ocean surf.

"You only wanna see steam coming off the top," he said, whipping the butter knife clockwise around the Pyrex. "If it starts to smoke or turn brown, that means you're burning it.

It could also mean your shit is cut with sugar, but you would know *that* from the caramel smell."

The song playing in the apartment was "Break Da Law" from the Mystic Stylez album, released in 1995. Juicy J, DJ Paul, Lord Infamous, Koopsta Knicca, Gangsta Boo, Crunchy Black—all the original members, doing what they do best. Worm loved the record, loved the heavy bass and eerie melodies.

"I'm just tryin' to give you a skill. If something happens to me, you won't be lost."

Break the law. Break the law. Break the law.

"Does it really smell like caramel?" asked Worm.

Ray whipped the knife. The morning sun leaked through the mini blinds in the space between the vinyl slats and burned tiger stripes of light across his tattooed forearm.

"Yes," he laughed. "It sure do."

Ray took the Pyrex out of the boiling water and turned the burner off. Worm thought of Twix and Snickers and Milky Ways and Milk Duds. Hunger burned blue in his stomach.

"Can we get pizza?"

The water in the Pyrex had evaporated. Ray took a glass of ice water out of the refrigerator and poured it in.

Ray smiled. "We'll see."

"And ice cream?"

Ray agitated the water, shaking the pot gently. "Maybe. I said *maybe.*"

Worm watched his father work. "I like salted caramel. That's my favorite ice cream."

"Listen," said Ray. "This time we spend together is important. One day I'm gone pick you up, put you down and never pick you up again. And then it'll just be you against the world. And the world is never gone pick you up. It'll be all on you, baby boy."

Worm looked at his fingernails and considered this.

Ray used a spoon to hold the hard, white chunks against the side of the Pyrex measuring cup. He tipped it over the sink, careful to only let the water drain out.

*"Grams go for $80 in the drought they $120,
but all my work good you can put some extra on it"*
- C Watt

10

When Worm woke up his lap was on fire. The creature was squatting in front of him, its hands between its legs, rubbing its crotch violently. It moaned in ecstasy as saliva dripped from the opening in its face. Worm felt around in his pocket with his free hand. The heroin. It was still there. He fondled the balloons in his pocket and waited.

When the creature leaned in again, he kicked out with his right leg and caught it in the stomach. Worm heard something inside of it snap. It toppled over towards him, its head falling into his lap, jagged mouth-hole open, gasping for air. In one fluid motion, Worm used his free arm to stuff the balloons down the creature's throat, then clapped his hand over its mouth-hole. He spun it around so that its neck was in the crook of his arm and squeezed as hard as he could.

He put all his weight into it. "Motherfucker."

The creature struggled for a bit, making animal noises underneath Worm's hand. Eventually, its legs kicked out, stiff in the air, then settled to the ground and stayed there. The air in the room stank of shit. Worm held his hand over its mouth for a while longer before letting go. He checked its pulse. Nothing. Still not satisfied, he seized its head with his free hand and twisted it to the side until he heard its neck snap. The sound echoed in the basement.

He used the fingers of his free hand to pry open the hole in its face. *Yep,* he thought. The balloons of dope had burst in the thing's throat, choking it on the grittiness of it. The creature was dead but Worm was still cuffed to the radiator. He pulled the thing's body closer. His fingers felt around, rummaging through the pockets of its jeans. He found nothing of use, came back with thick ropes of flesh that sloughed off the bone. A gold name necklace lay in the dip of the creature's throat.

Chanel.

Worm jerked his hand back. The thing was human once. *What happened here?*

Worm looked at his right wrist; the plastic zip tie cutting into his flesh. He had been in this position once before, a long, long time ago. Not in a rowhouse. But in a small apartment on the Eastside.

Ray was as good a father as any father in the early '90s could be. He made sure Worm had three solid meals a day. The air mattress had air in it and he could always find clean socks and underwear. There was reasonably clean drinking water. Before the first week of school, Ray would always come home with the newest Jordans and a few fresh outfits. Worm never had to start the school year in last year's clothes. That really made a difference to a kid.

They were watching television in the one bedroom apartment. Worm sat on the air mattress eating a steak and cheese eggroll. Globs of cheese and onions had dribbled down his chin and fallen onto the blue, plastic bed.

"Now, you know it's for your own good," Ray said, dangling a pair of handcuffs in front of him. "To keep you safe."

"But I don't want to," Worm pleaded. "It hurts."

"That shit don't hurt, boy. Stop being so dramatic."

"What if I have to pee?"

Ray used the toe of his sneaker to push a plastic trash can towards his son. "That's what the bucket for."

Many years later, Worm would learn to understand why his father did what he did. Rent and living expenses would cease to be intangible concepts. He would learn to understand that food doesn't mysteriously materialize in the refrigerator and nothing in life is free.

And so it went: the boy remained handcuffed to the stove while the father went down to the corner to sell drugs.

The sun went down outside. Ray had brought the TV into the kitchen so that Worm could see the screen. Worm twisted his handcuffed wrist around so that the joints crackled and popped. On the television, Jessie from *Saved By the Bell* got addicted to caffeine pills and an evil ventriloquist dummy named *Stevil* chased Steve Urkel around the house.

On *The Simpsons,* Principal Skinner discovered that the roast he was preparing burned. "Oh, egads! My roast is ruined!

But what if I were to purchase fast food and disguise it as my own cooking?"

It was very important that this plan worked. Principal Skinner had invited Superintendent Chalmers over for dinner; he had to make an excellent impression. This was Superintendent Chalmers after all.

Principal Skinner climbed out of his kitchen window and ran across the street to Krusty Burger. There, he brought hamburgers and french fries to replace his burnt roast. He entered the dining room with the fast food on a silver tray, ready to pass off the purchased fast food as something he had cooked himself.

"Superintendent, I hope you're ready for some mouth watering hamburgers," he said.

Superintendent Chalmers eyed him suspiciously. "I thought we were having steamed clams," he said.

Worm's mouth watered, too. He thought about double cheeseburgers with no pickles, no onions, add Mac sauce. That was the wave. That was how you had to do it. The Mac sauce set it off.

Martin was on TV making fun of Cole which meant it was 8:00 p.m. Cole glared back at him. "I'll see you in Hell, Martin"

Martin laughed. "Yeah, you'll be the only one down there still living with your mother."

His father had never left him in the house alone for this long. He always came home before Martin came on. Something was wrong. Worm shivered.

Martin reached inside Cole's chest and came back with his heart, bright red and still beating. His jaw dislocated and stretched out to impossible lengths. Gina put her head in first, then Pam. Martin chewed. Masticated human flesh fell out of his mouth.

The first night passed by in a blur of shadows that ran across the kitchen walls with claws and tentacles and proboscises. Hunger burned blue in his stomach. It started as a thin line in the shape of a circle that sat in the pit of his belly. The outline of the circle grew thicker, bolder. The circle would spin at various intervals. It would change colors. Pulse with the beat of his heart.

On the third night, Worm decided to break his thumb and escape the handcuff. Using his free hand, he pulled back on the thumb until he felt the ligaments tear. He was panting. This would be difficult. He would have to make it quick in order to successfully break the bone. Once the bone had been broken, the thumb could be positioned further in front of the palm, so that he could wiggle his smushed-together hand through the cuff.

Worm pulled back as hard as he could and broke the thumb bone. Fire shot up his arm, nearly causing him to pass out. The room wavered. Worm took a deep breath and pulled at the cuffs. His hand would still not fit through. He was going to have to break the pinky.

The little finger was easier. The bone snapped like a twig, the pain from that break overshadowed by the white hot fire that ran from his scaphoid to his trapezium. His thumb throbbed with the beat of his heart. It took a few tries but he was finally able to slide the handcuff off.

Worm would have to do this again.

Now. Here in this fucked up basement with this dead creature a foot away from his bleeding lap.

He studied his thumb, ran his fingers along the plastic of the zip tie. He pulled against the cuff. A creaking sound came from the radiator. Worm yanked on the tie again. Hard. Harder. The sound of popping metal came from inside the steel columns. He punched forward as hard as he could and ripped the radiator off the wall. The pipe-shaped metal that ran across the top of the columns had cracked through, allowing Worm to work the zip tie over and off the radiator. He stood up and stepped over the corpse of the creature.

When Worm opened the door at the top of the stairs the light blinded him. He covered his face and waited for his eyes to adjust. The first thing he saw was a body on the couch. His brain registered that it was a body, rather than a living person because the head had been crudely removed. He looked up and saw where the light was coming from. There was a hole in the ceiling of the rowhouse. *No,* he thought. *That's not quite right.* It was more than a hole in the ceiling. It was like the entire roof had been torn off the rowhouse. The big, hard Baltimore sun warmed his face. Ceiling beams lay on the hardwood floor.

And there was a body on the couch so he needed to keep it moving.

The black satchel and the keys to Sweet Breath's Lincoln were on the stove. Worm grabbed the keys and swung the satchel over his shoulder. He stopped when he saw the blue powder on the coffee table. At first, it looked like Oxy. He was all too familiar with crushed up M-Boxes, lined up in heaps and hills that looked like a topographical map of Appalachia. Whatever this was, it was something different. The powder refracted light. Rainbows stretched out from the blue pile like an oil spill. Worm stared at it, watching it turn and twist, the colors separating, then pulling back into the blue.

Later on, he would ask himself why he did what he did. He would not be able to explain why he did it. Not in words, anyway. He could not help himself, that he knew. Like some otherworldly force had compelled him. No words or expressions existed to describe the feeling. The intense need to do it. He dipped a finger into the blue powder and touched it to his tongue. Then, the world came unhinged.

Worm stood in an orchard. A cool breeze rustled the dark green leaves of the fig trees. He tasted salt, felt the ocean air against his bare chest. He plucked a swollen fig and bit into it, exposing the pink and yellow flesh. The flavors burst in his mouth and sent signals through his taste buds. Papaya. Honeydew melon. Guava.

A procession of men passed by, ignoring Worm. They wore black tactical gear and neoprene masks, polycarbonate smoke lenses that made them look like insects as they marched by. A man at the front of the line carried a long staff of giant fennel. Ivy vines ran around the length of it and terminated at the tip, where amber honey the color of a nocturnal animal's eyes dripped from a large pine cone. Worm followed behind them.

They walked until they came to the ruins of what was once an ancient temple or amphitheater. Kudzu crawled up the flutes of the Doric columns like varicose veins. Engravings of squid-like creatures were carved into the frieze of the entablature.

"Bring me the *kantharos*." The man that held the staff had removed his mask. Long, black hair fell to his shoulders. He was a tall man, well over six feet with a wide forehead and regal features. His dark, almond shaped eyes swirled as he watched the team of men before him.

Two soldiers opened a case to reveal a chalice with a deep bowl and tall pedestal foot. Loop-shaped, high-swung handles rose from the bottom of the body and extended high above the brim. Silhouettes of figures with horns and tentacles covered the body of the *kantharos* in the style of 5th century BC black-figure pottery.

"The god on the cross is a curse on life," said the man with the staff. "When life is about seeking redemption, how can one truly live?."

Within the ruins, a marble statue of one of the squid-like creatures loomed high above the men. The sunlight made the white stone shine with a faint golden tinge. He placed the chalice at the foot of the brobdingnagian statue. The ground began to shake. Worm watched as a mountain range of tubular polyps and tentacles rose from the earth within the ruins. Flesh blocked out the sky, tinting the orchard sarcoline. Red ichor flowed over the crumbling columns and travertine paving.

"Gather as much of it as you can," said the man with the

staff. The liquid flooded the olive grove, rolling over the roots and soil, splashing the undergrowth and pooling in thick, hematic puddles. "The blood has incredible properties."

The soldiers produced thick, rubber tubing that ran from their rucksacks, which they had lowered onto the ground. At the end of each tube, a cannula the size of a man's finger shined in the light, metal and sharp. The men jammed the tubes into the creature's body and began to siphon its blood. Deep blue ran through the tubing and disappeared into the rucksacks.

"I'm in the trap where the guns at"
- Blue Benjamin Sleepy

11

Then, he was standing on the sidewalk, in front of the rowhouse with the bombed out roof. The sun was oppressive; the heat, an act of aggression. Worm fell to his knees. The light of the outside world cut through his skull like an ice pick. More than ever, he wanted to retreat, go back in the rowhouse, lock himself inside and never come out. He wanted to cover himself in furniture and drapes, sheets and mattresses. He wanted to dig a hole through the floorboards of the living room and pack the hole with couch cushions and throw blankets. It would be a nest. He would spread his scent through the hole, touch everything and allow everything to feel him back. Then everyone would know it was *his* nest. Then, Simone would follow his scent, track him back to the rowhouse and join his nest.

He shook his head. He smacked himself in the face, twice across each cheek. He made a fist and punched his chest.

Need to get my mind right, he told himself and kept punching.

The back of his head burned. He stopped punching, reached back and felt wetness at the base of his skull. He winced when he pressed his fingers against it. His fingertips came back bloody and a wave of nausea made him keel over. The sun pressed him down, further to the ground until the knuckles of his bruised, right wrist grazed the sidewalk. He wrapped his left arm around his body and hugged himself.

Worm looked up and saw a man in a neon purple zoot suit dancing in front of a cherry dogwood. He bear-hugged an armful of cardboard boxes, overflowing with crumpled papers and clothing.

"My shit!" he barked. "Bitch tried to walk off with all my shit. Can you believe it? That dirty, no good bitch."

Holes had eaten through the man's shoes. He wobbled like an inflatable tube man, leaning to the left until it looked like he would fall over, then snapping back up, perfectly straight, standing at attention. He started to lean again, this time to the right. Worm watched as the man began to bend at the knee, as if he were about to bow, then kick his right leg out, then bend at the knee again, then kick his left leg out. He performed this dance, bouncing up and down like a rodeo clown.

A silver Delahaye 135 pulled to the curb and idled in front of the dancing man. Worm had never seen a Delahaye in real life. It looked out of place, like some kind of deep sea creature that had gotten itself lost in the photic zone. The word *Antioch*—with a cross in place of the letter T—was stenciled in crimson across the rear window.

Fuckin' Antiochians, Worm thought.

The suicide doors opened and two men in black, leather jumpsuits got out. Each wore a gimp mask with a zipper across the mouth, and black choker collars wrapped around their necks. Buckles and metal inlays were placed at seemingly random locations all over their bodies.

The man in the purple zoot suit didn't see them coming. By the time he stopped dancing it was too late.

"Check it out," the first gimp said, pressing a long finger into the purple zoot suit man's chest.

The second gimp nodded and pinched the man's cheek. The man shivered as the gimp rubbed his thumb and forefinger against his skin. "Not much left of him. Hardly worth the effort."

The purple zoot suit man seemed to shrink in the presence of the gimps. He looked at them pleadingly. "Bitch tried to walk off with all my shit. C-Can you believe it?"

The first gimp flicked a lighter and the loose papers hanging out of one of the man's boxes caught fire. The man in the purple zoot suit didn't react until the whole box of papers burst into flames, causing him to launch his possessions into the air. Gray newspaper ash and black fabric exploded all over the sidewalk.

The gimps threw back their heads and laughed at the sky. The man in the purple zoot suit crouched on the ground, trying to gather his belongings. The papers had all been destroyed but the clothing could still be salvaged.

Tears ran down the man's face. "All my shit! Look what you did with all my shit."

Worm rubbed his eyes and watched the second gimp crouch. The first gimp did a front flip and landed on the back of the second gimp. He pulled himself up until he was standing on the second gimp's shoulders. The second gimp lowered his center of gravity and gripped the first gimp's ankles to support him.

The first gimp pounded his chest and roared. "Ladies and gentleman, boys and girls, children of all ages, prepare to be amazed!"

The purple zoot suit man looked up at them. "My shit?"

Worm watched, frozen in disbelief, as the first gimp launched himself off the second gimp, diving into the disheveled man with his elbow cocked out. He heard the bones in the man's face crunch.

The first gimp got up and removed his mask. Long, rust-colored hair billowed out and Worm saw that the first gimp was female. "Get the manganese heptoxide," she said.

The man in the purple zoot suit lay prone on the ground, his facial features rearranged in abstract places like a Pablo Picasso painting; the nose where the cheek should be and the eyes all pushed to one side, almost to the point of being stacked on top of each other. The second gimp went to the silver Delahaye and returned with an oversized ampoule filled with dark green liquid. He cracked his neck and did a couple of jumping jacks. Then he broke the ampoule on the lifeless body and Worm watched in disbelief as the man in the purple zoot suit burst into flames. Within moments the corpse had blackened.

The female gimp did a backflip. "Sweet galactic Jesus! You really fucked him up!"

"He was dead before we got here. He didn't know it yet, but he was." The male gimp jogged to the passenger side of the Delahaye and got in. "Let's make like barbecue sauce and *dip!*"

The first gimp did a cartwheel over to the Delahaye and got behind the wheel. She gunned the ignition and made it come alive. The muffler barked and Worm watched the Delahaye pull away from the curb, the stenciled, red letters of the word *Antioch* like blood splattered across the rear windshield.

"I'm from the home of the Wire don't Stringer Bell me"
- Young Moose

12

What the fuck just happened? Worm thought. *What did I just see? Why didn't I do anything?*

But really, what could he do? And why would he? What could be gained from getting involved in other people's business besides trouble? The last thing Worm needed right now was trouble. He had only been out of prison for seven hours. The drug still churned in his bloodstream, his equilibrium was off and he knew he looked terrible. And what if they piss tested him at the halfway house tonight? Would this evil shit make him pop a positive? And what would it even show up as in the urinalysis results? He'd catch a parole violation immediately and be right back in the joint. And what then? No, he wasn't guilty of inaction, wasn't wrong for minding his business. The best way to stay out of trouble in this city was to not get involved.

The image of the first gimp diving off of the second gimp and elbow dropping into the purple zoot suit man's face stuck with Worm. He could hear the man's skull shifting, the sharp edges of broken bones scraping against each other and puncturing the flesh.

Worm unlocked the Lincoln and got in the driver's seat. It was all wrong. Everything. He had so much more legroom than when he first got behind the wheel. The roof seemed impossibly high; the steering wheel massive as the stainless steel wheel found in the helm of a sailboat. He extended his right leg, tried to touch the pedal. He couldn't reach it. The tips of his fingers grazed the steering wheel. He sunk in the bucket seat, the windows and sunroof encapsulating him like aquarium glass as the air rushed like water through his lungs.

Worm vomited. He rummaged through the glovebox, looking for napkins or something to wipe the mess out of his lap. Insects buzzed inside his head, sending back information, always transmitting something to somewhere. He used the owner's manual of the Lincoln to push off the vomit and cried out in pain.

"What the fuck?" He looked down at his lap, saw the bloodstain on his thigh, remembered how that *thing* had bit a chunk out of him, remembered how that *thing* that was probably human once had swallowed that piece of him, consuming a part of him. He felt around and saw that a small, but not insignificant part of his inner thigh was missing.

When Worm looked up from his lap he saw himself standing across the street, near the burnt body of the man in the purple zoot suit. But that was impossible. He was inside the Lincoln, sitting in the driver's seat, his lap on fire and pieces of vomit still stuck to his baggy jeans. And yet, there he was. Standing across the street; oversized white t-shirt hanging from a wiry frame, baggy jeans with a dark splotch over the right thigh. That was definitely him.

That's definitely me, he thought. *But if that's me across the street then who am I? Who is the one watching me from my eyes? Am I the me that's watching the me from the car or the me that's standing across the street?*

Worm pressed his palms into his eyes. When he opened them he saw that he was no longer standing across the street.

"That's what I thought," he said out loud.

The inside of the Lincoln went back to normal. It was just a normal car.

And I am not a good person.

The thought had been with him since he killed the thing in the house. *What type of people get involved in crazy, evil, fuck shit like that?* People like him apparently.

There was a time when he thought he might have done something with his life.

In school, maybe. Ninth grade, tenth grade, before he stopped going.

Mr. Draghoun would preach. "Nixon declared drugs public enemy number one. Reagan took that rhetorical war and made it a literal one. Incarceration rates soared. Systemic racism in the justice system and mandatory minimums put an obscene number of black people behind bars. More arrests meant more federal money. Federal job stimulus, millions in U.S. Department of Justice grants for crime control and community policing, all that. The game was rigged. It was never a war on drugs. It was a war on the black people of Baltimore."

"For sure," Worm nodded. "But that's just one part of it, right? There's also shit like how they made the roads all fucked up, how they went and ran that bullshit highway right through Harlem Park. How there ain't no grocery store in Sandtown. Just liquor stores and churches and beauty supply joints. That urban planning shit."

"Exactly," Mr. Draghoun said, putting his hands together. "You've been listening, learning, enlightening yourself. You're talking about spatial injustice."

"How folks who live over Westside have a life expectancy twenty years lower than the rest of the city."

"You know it, man. If we start with incomplete stories how can we ever find complete solutions?"

"Right."

"The problem is that nobody *thinks* they can make a difference," Mr. Draghoun would say. "So nobody *makes* a difference. It's that simple."

"But how?" Worm had skipped the whole day at school except Mr. Draghoun's class. Then he had come back after everyone had left the school, to talk with this interesting teacher from West Baltimore who was not like anyone he had ever met. Worm sighed. "I ain't got shit, I can't do shit."

Mr. Draghoun would just smile with his mouth closed, and then his eyes would flicker, just barely, which would confirm something to Worm that he already knew: nobody had anything figured out. Nobody. People had emotions and felt things about things and sometimes people surprised you. And when they did, it sure was nice, but mostly the world was fucked up and full of sharp edges, and nobody knew what the fuck they were doing.

"Me and my mother was poor,
We used to stay on the second floor,
She used to play with the raw,
She used to snort it up her nose with the straw"
- GGL Slick

13

It was November and the sun had already started to go down, painting everything mauve. The lights of the inner harbor glittered like diamonds in the distance. A group of black kids stood in front of Lanvale Towers. There were at least eight or nine of them, and all of their sneakers were glowing. Worm didn't understand what he was seeing, but goddamn if their feet weren't blocks of pulsating white light. As he got closer he realized what was happening. All of the young men wore the same shoes. Gray New Balance 994's. He was seeing the light bounce off the reflective New Balance logos.

The part of his thigh where the thing had taken a bite out of him burned hot. It would be infected soon if it wasn't already. *How much longer,* Worm mused, *can I go on like this?* and then, because he had no other choice but to keep going on like this, he pushed that thought down, deep down into a place where it was too dark for it to find him again.

The world is an awful place and there's not much anyone can do about it on a macro scale. But as long as you're alive, there's a chance to change and improve. And when you change yourself, you change the immediate world around you.

"We can't change the world on a macro scale," Mr. Draghoun would say. "But we can change it many, many times over on a micro one."

Worm made his decision.

The people of Baltimore had already been through enough. They didn't deserve this, whatever *this* was. He wasn't going to let this happen. He was going to stand up. He would do it for Simone and her baby, they deserved that, and if he ever really loved her he would make himself believe that he was happy for her until he believed it for real. And everybody else. It was hard out here. You couldn't have crazy, new drugs and maniacs in gimp suits terrorizing the city. It wasn't fair. There was already enough crazy evil out here.

He had to do something. He had to try, at least.

The city was special. In Baltimore, anything could happen. Anyone could become anything here. But more importantly, Baltimore represented Simone because Baltimore had created her. She was born here, raised here, even went to school here. Simone represented strength and perseverance and drive, and all the things he loved about Simone were the same things he loved about Baltimore.

But really, he was lying to himself. It wasn't because he respected the resilience of the city, or even that he wanted to protect Simone. Those were good reasons to have but they weren't his. He was far too selfish a person for that. It was all about survival.

Self-preservation.

Because he knew that he was never going to leave the city. It was crazy for him to even entertain the thought. Baltimore was the only city someone like Worm could make a life in. Baltimore was eclectic and tolerant of things other cities weren't. This was a place where he could start over. This was what he believed. Besides, he didn't know anything else. This was it.

One time Worm had been dropping a ten pack of 8mg Dilaudid off to a waiter at Michael's Cafe, an upscale steak and seafood joint in Timonium. Rich leather seats. Wood bar. Two entrances, hostesses at each end dressed in an all black with their hair immaculately done. Some of the diners wore suits and sports jackets, the women in black bandage dresses. But there were other people there in Adidas tracksuits, jeans and t-shirts, sneakers. Black folks, white folks, whoever. And nobody was passing judgment. Everyone ate in peace. Everybody eating there had to have money in order to spend it, and at that moment, they were all spending it together. It didn't matter what they were wearing. At that moment, everybody was celebrating and eating the same crab cakes. It was like the money and the fine dining made everyone similar enough to not see their differences, just for that brief moment. Worm did not believe that the rest of the world was like that. Baltimore had its problems, so many, but it was a place where you could make it from the bottom to the top.

You could also disappear.

He had made it to Sweet Breath's house, his head thumping and armpits damp. He parked the Lincoln behind the rowhouse and turned off the engine. Worm knocked on the door, stood back and clenched his fists.

"You're back." The fat man clasped his hands together and grinned like a Cheshire cat.

Worm didn't wait. He rushed in and threw an uppercut that lifted Sweet Breath off the floor. Blood spurted out of the fat man's mouth—the sound of teeth clicking echoed throughout the rowhouse. A framed poster of Enrique Iglesias fell off the wall.

"Not my Enrique!" cried Sweet Breath.

Worm could feel the chemical in his bloodstream. It crawled through his veins like bullet ants, the pain rushing through him, controlling his movements. He smashed the framed poster over the fat man's head.

Sweet Breath dropped like a bag of dirty laundry, his beehive hairdo unraveling as he hit the floor.

"Would you dance, if I asked you to dance?" he sang, more blood bubbling on his lips, "Would you run, and never look back?"

Worm drove an elbow into the fat man's face. Bone and cartilage crunched like celery. Worm took hold of his shoulders and shook him. "What did you do? What the fuck did you do?"

Sweet Breath spit out a tooth. "Settle down, my boy. I intend to compensate you, thusly."

Worm backhanded him across the face.

"Come on man!" Sweet Breath held up his hands. "I said *thusly.*"

"Yeah, you definitely gonna compensate me. In fact, let me get that $300 you owe me. Right now, right now. Shit, let's round that up and make it a flat G. What you think? That sound good to you, you fuckin' animal?"

"Fine, fine," said Sweet Breath, crawling over to the safe. He worked the combination lock and came back with a banded stack of hundred dollar bills. "We good then, my boy?"

"Fuck no." Worm took the stack and then kicked him in the stomach.

"Goddamn!"

"What is this shit?" Worm held the black satchel close to Sweet Breath's chin. "Tell me what it is."

"What shit, baby?"

Worm kicked him in the stomach again. Sweet Breath let out a yelp.

"It's the cosmic darkness, baby boy. Ain't nothin' to it but to do it."

"But why? Why would you make this?"

"Make?" Blood dribbled down the fat man's right cheek. "Fuck I look like? Bill Nye the Science Guy? Do I look like Breaking Bad to you?"

Worm smacked him in the face. "Why though? What's the point? Killing your customers? Why? For what?"

Streams of blood and perspiration ran down Sweet Breath's neck rolls. "Because I *can*. Mostly. And because it's funny. Sometimes, I put a GoPro with a live feed in the bag with the batch. You ever bust a nut to somebody gettin' their face peeled off?"

Worm put the jar down and fumbled around in his pocket. He came out with Sweet Breath's keychain and had an idea.

Quickly, he wedged three of the keys in the space between his fingers so that the shanks pointed out past his knuckles, like how women hold their keys when they have to walk back to their car alone in a parking garage at night.

"Look, you goofy fuck, I wanna know where this shit came from. Where it's coming from." Worm held his fist close to the side of Sweet Breath's face, the key tips mere millimeters from his eye. "I'll fucking blind you."

"Come closer," the fat man rasped.

Worm leaned in, his clawed fist close to Sweet Breath's temple.

Sweet Breath began to sing again. "I will stand by you forever. You can take my breath—"

Worm drove the keys into the fat man's eye. Blood misted out of Sweet Breath's orbital bone, followed by the collapse of his eyeball. When Worm withdrew his spiked fist, the fat man's egg yolk-colored sclera deflated.

Sweet Breath let out an animal-like shriek, reminding Worm of the time he found his older cousin torturing a cat behind the Quikway. His cousin Rico had trapped the poor animal in a fitted sheet and was swinging it around his head like a helicopter. Worm had begged his cousin to let the cat go, but that had only amplified Rico, hyping him up until he was swinging the cat faster and faster. Tears sprang from young Worm's eyes as Rico smashed the cat into the brick of the Quickway.

"Fuck man! My eye! You done took my eye!. It's never been done before. It hurts!"

"Their names. I want their names."

*"I'm from the Eastside of Baltimore you know where I be,
Bel Air Road, zip code 21223"*
- Dave The Barber

14

Worm had heard about the Greeks, the rumors about their savagery, so it made sense when Sweet Breath finally gave them up as the manufacturers of this dangerous new drug.

He knew he would need a better weapon than car keys and searched throughout the house for something more substantial to use against the Greeks. In the bathroom, he found a black felling axe. He picked up the lightweight, fiberglass handle and swung it through the air.

It was important to understand that the Greeks were not Greek people. Well, they were people who were Greek, but they were not *all* Greek people, obviously. There was talk about a specific group of gangsters from Greektown that pushed white ECP—Raw, Boy, King Heroin–out of a club on Newkirk Street called Carcosa. Worm laughed at the name.

Like Ambrose Bierce, that Robert Chambers King in Yellow shit, he thought. *How derivative.*

The Greeks.

Kings come and go.

Worm had a plug named Maury. The most reliable drug dealer in the history of drugs. $100 per gram of raw heroin, that golden, sand-like stuff that smelled like flowers and vinegar. Never a discount no matter the quantity but always reliable and available at all times.

There were periods of time when Worm had been on the run or in prison and lost contact with Maury but Worm could always depend on finding the plug on Instagram or whatever social network he was on, sending Maury a message and making it happen.

When Worm met Maury, he lived with somebody else on the first floor of a Federal Style rowhouse on Hollins Street over Southwest. He drove a 328, black with black rims, stayed with a fresh shape up and Balenciaga kicks, flexing on everybody. The BMW was a late model, though. The Balenciagas were the only pair he had.

Years passed. Worm watched the late model BMW turn into a Hellcat Redeye with Forgiato rims. The one pair of Balenciaga sneakers became the Triple S in all color combinations, the ones that look like something your dad might wear to mow the lawn. He moved out of the rowhouse over Southwest. Soon Worm was meeting him near Ice Queens in Locust Point, which meant he must have gotten a place there.

Then one day he was gone.

He stopped answering his phone, texts, Instagram direct messages. A month or so went by without him posting any pics on social media. Then six months. And that was that. He never heard from him or about him again. Worm always assumed he got locked up or killed. It didn't matter what happened. Just that kings come and go and no one is impervious to the sharp edges of life.

"You're going to see some stuff that's going to make it hard for you to smile"
- Tupac Shakur

15

Keeping the white sheets over their heads was non-negotiable.

"I insist upon it," said Obelix. "All of my guests do it this way. I do it this way. It's how it's done."

The Ortolans had been kept in small, covered cages, reacting to the darkness by gorging themselves on figs and millet seed, nearly tripling their bulk. It had been Arturo's job to dump the birds into the 55-gallon, steel oil drum, then pour bottles of Armagnac over them until the drum was overflowing with it. This served a dual purpose: the brandy drowned the birds and flavored them at the same time.

The Antiochian sat diagonally across from Arturo. His mask had been removed when he arrived; the pale, gray skin of his face a stark contrast against the black leather of his gimp suit. The man looked tiny in proportion to the live edge Bastogne Walnut dining table, his confused expression reflected in the bronzed glass. Arturo had chosen this position at the table—first referred to by the University of Vermont in a major study on non-verbal communication in human interaction as the "independent position"—to present himself as indifferent, lacking any interest in Obelix and the Antiochian's dialectic pursuits.

Arturo fixed the gun in his waist so that he could lean back without the barrel putting pressure on his groin.

"What's up with the sheets?" asked the Antiochian.

Obelix selected one of the tiny, roasted birds and held it in front of his lips. "To shield us from the eyes of God, of course. That we should be ashamed to be seen participating in such a depraved activity."

The Antiochian studied the small bird on his plate. "I don't see the appeal."

Obelix's eyes suddenly grew cold. "Put it in your mouth."

"Say it again?"

"Feet first. Hold it by the head."

The Antiochian raised an eyebrow. "I ain't doing that shit."

Obelix reached under the table and came back with a loaded crossbow. He laid it on the table, light reflecting off the steel broadhead tip that was aimed directly at the Antiochian's chest. "I won't ask again."

The Antiochian seemed to consider this for a moment, then furrowed his brow. He put the Ortolan in his mouth—feet first—and bit down.

"I didn't know they could eat," Arturo said.

"Do you taste the flesh?" Obelix asked. "The fat and the sweetness of it? This is the opportunity I gave you. Because I am generous. Now put the whole thing in your mouth, damn it. I should see only the beak poking out between your lips."

The Antiochian packed the rest of the bird into his mouth until his cheeks swelled. A thin line of yellow juice ran down his chin. Arturo watched in disgust.

"Ah yes," said Obelix, grinning. "Now we are in the storm. Right in the eye of it. The bitterness you taste now is from the contents of the internal organs as they explode in your mouth. This represents suffering. Agony. The same agony that I felt when I found out you were cutting my product, diluting its potency, making it weak. And for what? Pocket change? *Efaga porta.* The bitterness of betrayal."

And there it is, thought Arturo. *All killings serve a dual purpose: to address imbalances and as opportunities to create art.*

"Now chew," commanded Obelix.

The Antiochian worked his jaws, crunching down on the entirety of the bird. Tears flowed freely down his cheeks.

Obelix chuckled. "As the fragile bones break on your teeth, and the sharp edges of those bones cut up your gums, I ask you, can you taste the metal of your own blood on your tongue? Can you taste it, salting the meat?"

The Antiochian nodded, his eyes wet and reflecting light.

"This is your redemption. This is you and I coming out of the storm. Together."

Slowly, the Antiochian swallowed. Arturo watched. Twice, the masticated bird almost came back up, but the Antiochian persevered, gulping it back down.

Obelix nodded at Arturo. He knew what to do.

Arturo placed a gun in front of the ashen-faced Antiochian—a heavy, Sig Sauer P365 that he had confiscated from the Antiochian while patting him down earlier. He was still swallowing when a confused expression washed over his face.

Obelix stroked the foregrip of the crossbow. "You will now place this gun, your gun, in your mouth, barrel first. This is similar to what we just experienced together with the Ortolan, yes?"

Arturo got up from the table. He would need to find some tarp, or perhaps some large lawn bags would do.

Obelix sat up and stroked the crossbow faster. "You will raise up this hammer of justice and you will insert its barrel into your mouth. You will taste the cold metal and you will pull that trigger back when I tell you to. You will take your own life at my behest. And if not, I will murder everyone who ever meant anything to you. I will murder all of your ridiculous friends in their leather and spandex nonsense. Even you Antiochians must have mothers, yes? Sisters? I will cut them up, defile their bodies in front of you. Make you watch as I open them up. I will be the end of all of you. Wiped from the earth without a trace. And then, I will murder you too, obviously."

The Antiochian pissed himself. "Please, don't kill me. Please."

"I hope not to have to resort to that," replied Obelix. "If you have been paying attention, then you understand that I have no desire to kill you. My wish is for *you* to kill yourself *malaka*. Willingly. For the sake of your family. Think of them, yes?"

"Please."

Obelix sighed. "What more can be done? *Den mas ekatse.*"

In the end, the Antiochian took his own life, just as Obelix had wished. Arturo wiped brain matter off the surface of the Bastogne Walnut dining table, making a note to himself to keep tarp—or perhaps some large lawn bags—in a more accessible location.

Obelix groaned. "That was depressing."

"The Antiochian's death failed to live up to your theatrical standards?" Arturo asked.

Obelix dropped ice cubes in a tumbler, poured clear liquid from a crystal decanter. "Us Greeks have a tradition of killing as an art form. It's in our mythology. Sinis, who tied people between bent over pine trees and later released them, ripping men in half; Sciron, who forced his victims to wash their feet before pushing them off a cliff; Cercyon, who killed those he defeated in wrestling matches, and so forth and so on. For us, murder has always been a medium for creative self-expression."

Obelix finished his drink, the look on his face a dour one.

"You could always desecrate the body," Arturo suggested, refilling Obelix's tumbler. "Quarter and section it. Carve a message into the flesh, perhaps? Leave it in the streets for everyone to see, to serve as a warning, maybe?"

Obelix waved his hand dismissively. "Ah! This suggestion of yours is not art. It would be visceral, yes, but one can find no interiority in the act of desecrating a corpse. It is only the act of killing itself through which an artist can transcend. A true artisan knows that the theater of killing is the *only* place in the world where a gesture, once made, can never be made the same way twice."

Arturo continued his attempts to dislodge a piece of the Antiochian's skull that had embedded itself in the burgundy upholstery of a diamond tufted chaise lounger.

"I'm from Baltimore, Maryland home of the heroin"
- 100 Grand Man

16

In the living room of a rowhouse in East Baltimore, Sweet Breath opened his remaining eye. At first, he could not move. Eventually, he made his way to the kitchen, using his arms to pull the rest of his body across the linoleum.

It took almost an hour for him to make it to the basement door, another ten minutes to get the door open. He crawled down the stairs, half-rolling his body and using his good leg—the one with the foot still attached to it—to push himself forward and down. He was unable to reach the pull string for the single bare bulb that hung from the ceiling; the grayish-blue glow that came in through a tiny window was the only source of light in the cramped basement.

In one corner of the room, a Sarcos Robotics exosuit hung from the ceiling. Sweet Breath had spent his last to acquire the powered exosuit. It had been modified to accommodate his massive frame; the metal stretched and bent so that he could fit inside the suit. The left leg had been altered so that it ended in a robotic foot, a prosthetic of sorts that Sweet Breath could move and manipulate the leg of the suit with.

It took even longer for Sweet Breath to lift his body into the suit; longer still to get his arms through the sleeves and his legs secured by the metal clamps.

"Back before these whores took my foot," Sweet Breath said to no one, "I had a problem with this dummy who owed me money. He was honest in the sense that he admitted that he had gotten high on his own supply. So he fucked my money up. All up. Inconsiderate. So damn inconsiderate, I know. I know this."

He powered on the exosuit and attempted to move the robotic arms.

"According to the Diagnostic and Statistical Manual of Mental Disorders, addiction is a disease. Diseases are things that people do not put upon themselves. People believe addiction is like this."

He wiggled the titanium fingers, made a fist, extended the thumb and index, touched the finger pads together to make an OK gesture.

"Anyway," he continued, "I don't give a fuck about none of that. Junky ass bitch. If you fuck my money up, it's go time. This dummy had kids. Two of 'em, boy and girl. The boy was like four, maybe five, and the girl was also young, but she was old enough to understand exactly what was happening to her and her brother. The boy, her brother, well, he kept asking questions. Always wanting to know what was happening, where his daddy was, when they could go home, and all that there. The girl, she just kinda sat there on the bed making these horizontal-pupil-eyed animal noises. Hugging her knees to her chest, rocking and whimperin and such."

Welded to each robotic arm of the exosuit were MK 153 anti-armor rocket launchers—long, green pipes that hung from mounting brackets. Attached to the back was an oversized needlegun, modeled after the ASM-DT underwater assault rifle. The 5.45mm flechette ammunition had been milled—long, imperfect grooves ran down the length of the spikes to retain the nerve agent VX, or some other neurotoxin that the fat piece of shit had paid to have them dipped in.

"She knew what was bout to happen. So I take out my stick, start going at it, stroking it up and down tryna get it ready for business. The little boy, he starts getting louder, talkin' 'bout, 'He's got a big snake! Look at it gettin' bigger! You see it? What's he doing with it?' and I just keep tugging. And the girl, she just keeps making those animal noises."

Sweet Breath studied the rocket launchers attached to his robotic arms. "The little animal noises got to fuckin' with me, fuckin' with my stick. The girl just hugging her knees and mewling all pathetic-like. I hit her a few times to make her stop, then she just sat there, and her eyes ain't really have nothing in 'em no more."

Sweet Breath stewed in a cloud of hate, craving violence, longing for barbarity. A red aura glowed around the frame of the exosuit. His teeth ached with the desire to bite down on something thick, meaty, something he could tear and rip chunks out of like a Kodiak bear, spitting out gristle and snapping back flesh.

"And right when I'm 'bout to put it in, her little brother start talkin' with the voice of God. And the reason I know it was the voice of God is because all of a sudden this little white boy was speaking in Yorùbá and everybody know that God is Nigerian. I know you know that."

The interloper had taken his eye and his Lincoln. He ground his molars together and tasted blood seeping through the gaps in his front teeth. His unmanaged blood sugar levels were driving him mad.

"So I don't speak none of that fufu jollof rice shit, but I understands him, see? He speaking in a different language but I'm hearing him in regular old English inside my ears, you dig? In the back of my throat and shit. He tell me how *love* is passive because love accepts things. But whole time, *will* is active because it changes things. So you gotta live with love under your will. You gotta set boundaries on how you receive love through an act of will. That's what he told me. The little white boy with the Nigerian accent. I damn near wasn't able to get the job done. Folks that know what I'm talkin about know what I'm talkin about."

Sweet Breath wiggled the mechanized prosthetic that was attached to the ankle of his amputated foot.

"I grab a sixty-two and break it down to fifty fifties"
　　　　　　- Sonny Gramz

17

The Greeks sat in the outdoor dining area in front of Carcosa, one-fisting *xtapodi* into their mouths. The grilled octopus looked like entrails; purple and slick.

"This is why you must stay away from American women," said one of them, flashing a mouthful of gold, diamond cut fronts. "These young American women are not the same. The place to go is Santorini. This is an island of course, small, but full of women with money and class and good breeding, yes? Clean women. So clean. You can stick your finger in their assholes, pull it out and no shit! No shit at all."

The man who was speaking—a cinereous specimen in his late sixties—waved his index finger so everyone could see. "No shit at all!"

One of the younger men drank from a bottle of Tsantali, throwing his head back then gulping. "Bullshit."

"*Bullshit*, he says." The older man pointed at the younger one, belting out laughter. "*Gamisou*! This *moonopano* gives his women the kiss of death, yes?"

The waiter—a young Greek, stocky with jet black hair—brought more bottles of Ouzo. "The kiss of death?"

The older man slapped the waiter on the back. "Yes! The kiss of death," he said, grabbing a bottle of Tsantali. "Kostas, tell him what this is."

The waiter grinned. "What is it?"

The younger man, Kostas, sighed and ran stubby fingers through his thick curls. "When you are going down on a bitch, you blow into her *mouni.*"

Kostas touched his fingers together and blew into the waiter's face. The Greeks erupted into rumbustious laughter.

The waiter laughed nervously and backed up a step. "What? Why?"

Kostas rolled his eyes. "For art. The air enters the bloodstream through the intrauterine wall and goes straight to the heart. Death is immediate."

The color drained out of the waiter's face.

"You see, Kostas?" said the older man, pointing at the ashen-faced waiter, laughing. "He is not a fan of your, how you say, *kiss of death.*"

Kostas turned to the waiter. "Maybe I could give your mother a kiss, no?"

The waiter sputtered an apology and retreated.

Worm watched them from across the street, low in the bucket seat of Sweet Breath's Lincoln Mark VIII. Just a few guys kicking it in the outdoor dining area of Carcosa. One of them was old. Another three were young. And two of them were big.

Real big.

Worm got out of the car. He breathed in the air, savoring the pungent, metallic, ozone flavor. Electric sparks danced on the back of his tongue.

He swung the axe over his shoulder and crossed the street. The Greeks sitting in front of Carcosa stopped eating and put their drinks down. The old man, the oldest of the Greeks, abruptly got up from the table and put his fedora on.

"*Ai Gamisoo*!" he said, spreading his fingers and extending them. He held his palm out in the faces of the other Greeks, giving them the *moutza*. "*Oríste*. I'm out of here."

Worm watched the old man power walk down the block.

The one named Kosta stood up and took his black and gold Clubmasters off. "What's this?"

Worm hadn't thought about his own appearance since putting on his baggy clothing at Central Bookings. He must have looked awful. A bloodstain the size of a dinner plate spread across his crotch and thigh. Eyes wild from tasting the mysterious blue powder. Thirty-six inches of hickory propped over his shoulder; big, black, double-bit axe head. He looked like an extra in a zombie apocalypse movie. Like he had walked out of hell and went straight to Greektown without making any pit stops along the way.

He swung the axe and took the man's head off, but not completely.

The blade must not have been sharp enough. Kostas' head lopped to the side, dangling by a flap of skin and muscle as thin as a skirt steak, the blade of the axe buried in his neck.

His body teetered, then fell backwards to the ground, taking the axe with him.

Two of the men—broad shouldered, with eyes set deep under Neanderthal brows, one bald and one with a tattoo of a poppy below his right eye—got up from the table. Their fists were like Christmas hams. He darted towards them and threw an uppercut away under the jaw of Face-Tattoo, lifting him off his feet. He fell on his ass, his chin hitting his chest with the sharp click of teeth connecting with teeth. He lay on the ground and stayed there.

The second came for Worm; head down, arms up, bobbing and weaving in a sit-down low guard. Worm threw wild crosses and jabs, pummeling the man; bone and cartilage crumpling under his fists like papier-mâché masks. The bald man fell to the ground, blood running from his nose and mouth.

A fiery pain lit up Worm's scalp. Face-Tattoo had grabbed a handful of his hair and was pulling him back. He dug the heels of his state-issued work boots into the street.

"You fuck!" screamed the Greek. "Obelix will skin you alive!"

Worm got down in a crouch. Lowering his center of gravity allowed him to reach both arms behind him and hoist the larger man over his back. For a moment they hung there—two men, the smaller one appearing to be giving the larger one a piggyback ride, in broad daylight, in the middle of Baltimore. Worm thought of his prison workout routine; the burpees, the squats, the lunges. He stood up straight, flipping the man over so that he was upside down in front of him with his head between his thighs.

"He's going to pile drive him!" someone shouted.

Worm dropped to the ground. The sound of a head of lettuce being crushed echoed through the streets of Greektown. He got the body off of his legs and shoved it to the side.

Worm pulled the axe out of Kosta's neck and pushed past the terrified waiter.

*"I'm from the Eastside, you know what kind of shit I'm on,
But I be everywhere, I sold drugs in Woodlawn"*
- Tate Kobang

18

Inside Club Carcosa, a naked woman in a witch's bridle danced atop a rotating Corinthian pillar. The whites of her eyes reflected light, her expression inscrutable behind the iron hoops that formed a cage around her head. The spiked bridle bit pressed down on her tongue, causing her to drool. The bass thumped. Worm recognized the song as a slowed-down version of True Faith by New Order. The woman left purple trails in the air as she gyrated on the platform.

I used to think that the day would never come.
I'd see delight in the shade of the morning sun.

Everyone had an aura here, including Worm. His was baby blue, the color of 30mg Oxycontin, and it radiated around his body like a two inch thick, luminous silhouette.

Or, he told himself, *maybe I'm tripping, probably still have that shit in my system.*

The lighting in the dancehall strobed, pulsing with the drum beat. The walls of the club were made of black velvet, or some kind of dark, fuzzy material. Worm let his fingers graze the wall, then pressed his palm against the cool material.

Ever since he tasted the blue powder at the house, ever since he had connected with whatever plane of existence the foul shit had come from, he had been overwhelmed with the urge to touch everything. The need to feel or clutch or handle something tangible, something solid. Textures. Touch. The cold, buttery smoothness of leather, the dusty, dry touch of summer sidewalks at dusk, the edges of things blurred, soft surfaces, as if you could lay down in them.

My morning sun is the drug that brings me near.
To the childhood I lost, replaced by fear.

Worm realized he had closed his eyes.

Get your head together.

He stretched his eyelids, wiggled his eyebrows up and down. How could simply tasting that blue shit fuck him up so badly? He raised his eyebrows again, stretching the skin of his forehead until it felt like wax paper, then took in his surroundings.

Flat screen TV's mounted behind a bar that stretched around the perimeter played a mix of public access infomercials and Eastern European snuff films. A dentist described his approach to patient care while a woman in a floral house dress was sodomized by a man covered head to toe in prison ink. The camera zoomed in to a close up of the inside of someone's mouth. The tattooed man raised a machete above his head and continued thrusting.

Mounted high on the walls, but below the televisions, were

the heads and skulls of various animals, some easier to identify than others. He recognized some of the humanoid mounts as slightly smaller than adult humans, not fully formed.

Children?

One of the mounts appeared to be a human head with a separate horse's head growing out of the side of its neck. Another looked like a bear, but unlike any bear Worm had ever seen before. Its fur was mangy, its mouth stretched far across its wide face. The eyes had no pupils—white globes that glimmered like marinated mozzarella balls.

Three Antiochians sat on a black, leather sectional, their attention focused on a board game of some kind, set up on the marble and glass coffee table in front of the couch. Two were dressed in the same style as the ones he had seen kill the mentally ill man on Woodholme—leather bodysuits and gimp masks, sharp, jagged zippers where the mouths should have been. The third Antiochian was shirtless. Gold hoops the size of door knockers hung from his nipples. A gold, Cuban link chain connecting the piercings slapped against his shiny, gray flesh. He wore a rubber Beyoncé mask; one bloodshot eye flickered back and forth behind the eye holes. The mouth of the mask hung open, almost erotically, as if begging for someone to put something inside of it.

I don't care 'cause I'm not there.

And I don't care if I'm here tomorrow.

The Antiochian with the die in his fist screamed. "You goofy fuck! I'll shove this game down your throat and set you on fire. You fuck!"

The fat one with the Beyoncé mask stood up from the table, knocking the board and miniatures to the floor. "Lepex, please. I implore you to remain calm."

The other Antiochian, the one still sitting, detached from this conflict between the other two, unzipped the mouth opening in his mask and drank from a bottle of D'Usse. He wagged his finger at them. "Cooler heads will prevail gentlemen."

"You know me, Pradeep. My head is always cool. *Always.*"

"Cool as the other side of the pillow, huh?" The one named Pradeep offered up this euphemism, timidly, like it was an experimental dish that he was sharing at a dinner party.

Beyoncé Mask winked through one of the eyeholes. "Cool as a polar bear's toenails."

The one called Lepex jumped up and prodded Beyoncé Mask in the chest with a black gloved finger. "Enough already with the polar bears! I insist on being taken seriously. What I should do, is I should cut a hole in your fat neck and fuck it!"

Beyoncé Mask grabbed Lepex by the throat with one hand and unzipped the mouth opening of his mask with the other. He pushed his massive fist into Lepex's mouth until the Antiochian's jaw spread wide, cracking and tearing. The sound was like a towel ripping. Beyoncé Mask continued to push, grinding his fist deeper until his entire forearm was inside of Lepex. He withdrew his arm with a wet, sucking noise and held out a fistful of viscera. The Antiochian's body fell to the side, clattering on the ground in a cacophony of metal studs and rings.

Worm thought about the man on the bus, the one who gouged his own eye out. *It's the cosmic darkness,* he had said. *Can you see it?*

Worm could see it now. He believed.

The New Order song was coming to an end.

A large projector screen fell from the ceiling. The two remaining Antiochians—Pradeep and Beyoncé Mask—immediately sat back on the couch. The body of the third Antiochian—Lepex—lay at their feet leaking blood. They stared at the screen, transfixed by whatever was about to happen. Worm heard the click and whir of a projector coming to life. The Antiochians cheered as a man in a hazmat suit appeared on the screen.

"Functional imaging in human test subjects suggests that specific phobias are neuroanatomically mediated. That is to say, the reaction to the subject of the phobia itself is either mitigated or exacerbated by limbic and paralimbic circuitry including the amygdala, anterior cingulate, insula and dorsolateral prefrontal cortex. These brain regions are involved in the representation and interpretation of the phobic object, in amplification of the phobic response, and generation of the characteristic somatic correlates of extreme fear."

The man on the screen removed his reading glasses, cleaned them, put them back on and continued his lecture.

"We have been looking very closely at our test subjects with Urbach–Wiethe disease. Although the dermatological changes are the most obvious symptoms, many of our patient volunteers have symptoms of a neurological nature. All of our volunteers show bilateral symmetrical calcifications on the medial temporal lobes. These calcifications affect the amygdala, which is responsible for processing biologically relevant stimuli, particularly those associated with fear. It should be noted that all of our invasive and non-invasive scans have shown a correlation between amygdala activation and episodic memory for emotional stimuli. Therefore, Urbach–Wiethe disease volunteers with calcifications and lesions in these regions suffered extreme impairments in these systems."

Two burly attendants in starched white uniforms emerged from behind the man, each wheeling a bariatric gurney in front of them. Worm could see they were in a sterile room with white walls and medical equipment. On one gurney was a white woman, early twenties, moderately attractive, eyes closed, sleeping maybe. Laid out on the other stretcher was a living skeleton, emaciated and shriveled, its lips pulled back to reveal teeth too big for its face. Some kind of dermatological aberration covered its naked body.

The man waved away the attendants and continued. "When exposed to dangerous stimuli, volunteers with amygdala lesions"—he motioned to the unconscious man on the gurney—"displayed a lack of the behaviors normally associated with the action program of fear."

What the fuck is this? Worm wondered, unable to look away from the events transpiring on the oversized projector screen.

The man in the hazmat suit gestured towards the woman on the opposite table. "Our test subject has a perfectly functioning amygdala, just like you or I. For our test, we will conduct a comparable approach by directly confronting our patient with fear-inducing stimuli and observing her behavior while also querying her subjective state. You can wake her up now Bieslicht."

Smelling salts were employed and the larger of the two attendants—the man named Bieslicht— cracked open a glass ampoule of ammonium carbonate in front of the woman's face, abruptly waking her. She moaned. Disoriented, she sat up in the gurney and realizing she was nude from the waist up, covered her breasts. The withered husk of a man on the table next to her did not move or speak. It was unclear to Worm if he was alive or dead.

"Bieslicht," commanded the man in the hazmat suit. "The instrument if you please."

The attendant presented a chrome briefcase and popped open the clasps. The camera pulled back and Worm could see that yes, the recording was in an operating theater. Over a dozen men and women in white hazmat suits surrounded the gurneys, watching whatever kind of procedure was being performed take place.

Seeing the crowd of physicians surrounding her for the first time, clipboards and pens out, watching and taking notes, the woman asked in a hoarse voice, "Where am I? What the fuck is this?"

Bieslicht removed something from inside the case and handed it to the man in the hazmat suit. When he lifted the object into the air there was a flash of steel and white polymer and all was revealed; a Magnum Research BFR single action pistol.

"This is a forty-five caliber revolver. Fully loaded," said the man in the hazmat suit, and when he said the word *loaded* he waved the pistol in the direction of the woman. "Restrain the test subject please."

The woman was still sitting up on the gurney. Her eyes muddled with confusion as Bieslicht grabbed her by the shoulders and slammed her down on her back, pressing her body into the mattress. When the attendant pulled the first restraint across her chest she began to scream, kicking her legs and flailing her arms. One of her kicks caught Bieslicht in the mouth before he could get the leg restraints secured and Worm found himself cheering for the woman. Blood poured from Bieslicht's split open lip.

The man in the hazmat suit ignored the struggle going on behind him. "Now I will demonstrate that the instrument is fully functional."

He opened the cylinder, removed all but one of the cartridges, made it spin and snapped the cylinder back into place. Now the woman was fully restrained, the leather straps pulled tight across her waist, knees and forehead. Black electrical tape wrapped around her face and the back of her head multiple times, sealing her mouth shut. Her bloodshot eyes rolled wildly.

The other attendant—not Bieselicht—placed a wire speculum on the woman's face to retract her eyelids and hold them open. The man in the hazmat suit pointed the gun at the shriveled husk, unconscious on the gurney.

He pulled the trigger and nothing happened.

The woman exhaled through her nose. A nose sigh, no, a nose *gasp* of relief,

The man in the hazmat suit pulled the trigger again.

Click.

And again. *Click.*

And yet again. *Click.*

On the fifth pull, Worm watched the shriveled man's face explode and be instantly replaced by something broken and incomplete; brain matter gray against white bone fragments and dark, red blood. The woman stopped squirming under her restraints and froze, her eyes wide with shock.

Worm licked his lips.

The woman in the gurney opposite the dead man began to scream through the electrical tape again. She struggled against her restraints, her shoulders straining, veins popping out of her forehead.

"Yes!" the man in the hazmat suit cried. He pointed at the terrified woman. "Take note of the subject's fear response, yes? Quite natural of course."

The music had stopped playing and Carcosa filled with the sound of the woman's muffled screams, suffocated and cut short by the electrical tape.

"Yes! Look at her little amygdala go! Her brain becomes hyperalert, pupils and bronchi dilate, her breathing accelerates. Her heart rate and blood pressure rise. Blood flow and streams of glucose to the skeletal muscles increase. Her gastrointestinal system slows down. Yes!"

The woman continued to scream with a mouth full of electrical tape.

"Now," said the man. "Observe."

The other attendant—not Bieselicht—held out another chrome briefcase, this one larger than the one that held the gun. He opened it up, removed some kind of instrument, something metallic and heavy. Leading from the instrument back to the briefcase were bipolar cautery cords. The man in the hazmat suit took the instrument in both hands, rotated a dial and unfolded the wirestock. The surfaces of the device were covered with what appeared to be circuitry.

Worm watched the man push in the rear trunnion, causing a long graphite cylinder to come out the front, the tip of which glowed blue with heat. The cylinder began to spin and the man in the hazmat suit positioned the rotating electrode tip in front of the woman's right eye, which darted all over the room, the eyelids pulled back by the speculum.

He flipped a switch on the side of the instrument.

Nothing happened.

The operating theater was silent, save for the whistling sound of the woman's frenzied attempts at breathing through her nose with the electrical tape blocking her mouth.

Suddenly, the Ginsu knife slicing sound of metal sliding against metal reverberated through the icy silence of Carcosa and the graphite cylinder doubled in length, impaling the woman through the eyeball. The test subject went unconscious and the cylinder retracted, springing back into the barrel with a metallic click.

"The Schepens scleral depressor if you will," beckoned the man in the hazmat suit and the attendant that was not Bieslicht handed him a small thimble shaped object. Light reflected off of steel as he inserted the tip of the depressor between the woman's globe and orbit. The space occupied by the probe displaced the retina inward and created an elevation, causing the eyeball to bulge outward.

The man in the hazmat suit addressed the audience. "The test subject's amygdala has been removed via electrofulguration. Using radio frequency alternating current, we have learned to heat the tissue by intracellular oscillation of ionized molecules. This will result in an elevation of intracellular temperature. When the intracellular temperature reaches sixty degrees celsius, instantaneous cell death occurs."

"What the fuck?" This time Worm spoke out loud.

"Quiet!" hissed the Antiochian named Pradeep. Beyoncé Mask turned to face Worm. The large man removed his rubber mask and pointed to his right eye socket. Black burn marks surrounded the empty hole. The other eye was fine and studied Worm lazily. A thin rope of saliva dripped from the corner of his mouth like translucent vermicelli. Worm sucked his teeth and turned back to the projector screen

The man in the hazmat suit turned to Bieselicht who handed him another chrome briefcase. From this third valise came a set of electrosurgical forceps with a foot pedal generator. Bieselicht laid the foot switch before the man's feet and backed away. The cords that ran from the foot pedal to the titanium handpiece hung loose with slack. The man in the hazmat suit stepped on the foot pedal and the electrodes at the tip of the forceps started to glow blue.

"If the tissue is heated to ninety-nine degrees celsius, the simultaneous processes of tissue desiccation and protein coagulation occur. Appropriately applied, desiccation and coagulation result in the occlusion of blood vessels and halting of bleeding."

As he pontificated on the multiple modalities which utilize electricity to cause thermal destruction of tissue, the man in the hazmat suit utilized the forceps on the test subject, working the glowing electrodes around her zygomatic arch and maxilla. There was sizzling and popping, reminiscent of the sound of bacon frying.

Worm smelled burning plastic and saw that the Antiochians were freebasing.

On screen, the man in the hazmat suit aimed the forceps at the location of the empty orbital bone where the test subject's right eye used to be. "Notice the dark textures caused by tissue carbonization."

Worm's mouth went dry.

The man in the hazmat suit gestured for Bieslicht to approach him. He handed the large attendant the electrosurgical forceps. "As eschar builds up on the tip, electrical impedance increases and this can cause arcing, sparking or ignition of the eschar. When cleaning the electrodes, the eschar should be wiped away using a sponge rather than the common scratch pad, because these pads will scratch grooves into the electrode tip. This will increase the build up of dead tissue."

After he finished cleaning the electrodes, Bieselicht returned the forceps and generator to the briefcase and the man in the hazmat suit requested additional smelling salts to revive the test subject. Bieslicht carefully removed the electrical tape from the woman's mouth, the leather restraints unbuckled and left hanging off the sides of the bariatric gurney. A glass ampule broken below the woman's nose caused her eyes to flutter open. The man in the hazmat suit drummed his fingers on the sides of his lab coat and whispered the word *observe*.

"Where am I?" the woman asked.

"You are in an operating room my dear," the man in the hazmat suit informed her. "You have no cause for concern and are in the best of hands. We have removed your amygdala and you no longer have anything to fear."

Bieselicht stood behind the man, a goofy smile plastered across his oversized moon face.

"My amyg-whatta?" the woman asked. "Do I need that?"

The camera pulled back again and all around, smiles appeared on the audience of lab coat-ensconced professionals faces and the room was filled with boisterous laughter. The man in the hazmat suit applauded, holding his hands out palm-side up, as if to say *I told you so*.

"What's wrong with my eye?" the test subject said to herself quietly, then louder, "What did you do to my eye?"

"Ah yes, " the man in the hazmat suit said with a tired sigh. His words dripped with artificial sincerity. "In order to remove the amygdala we had to utilize the right orbital bone as the point of entry. Unfortunately, the eye was sacrificed in order to do so. I assure you, it is better this way. You won't even miss it."

"Oh shit," said the test subject, her voice calm and steady.

She seemed calm. Completely at peace. No visible signs of concern with what should be the trauma-inducing discovery of her permanent partial blindness. Worm didn't get it.

The corners of her mouth turned up into a goofy smile. "That's fucked up, man."

Another round of laughter and applause erupted from the jovial audience of physicians. Then the projector clicked off and the screen snapped back up into the ceiling. The show was over.

Worm rubbed his eyes. Nothing made sense. Everything had changed while he was locked up. There was nothing here for him in Baltimore anymore. This was not *his* city.

The two Antiochians were no longer seated on the sectional and the body of the third had been removed. The woman in the witch's bridle had also disappeared. The Corinthian pillar she had been dancing on rotated slowly, whirring as it turned. Worm was surprised he hadn't noticed them leave.

Then the vents opened up and released the carfentanil gas, knocking out Worm and making him smell baby powder on his way down to the floor.

*"Over East certified yeah that's where I remain,
You from West lil nigga look stay in your lane,
I ain't with this rap beef I'll put your face in a frame,
How you let a nigga put you out your own campaign?"*
- Young Moose

19

It was hard to know if he was alive or dead. The upper right half of his face felt cold, and something warm flowed freely from his forehead, burning his eye and blurring his vision.

Eye.

The taste of blood filled his mouth and nose until he had to lean forward and cough it up in order to keep breathing.

Eye.

Strangely, he felt at ease.

When he realized he was only looking at the world through his left eye he already knew what had happened. "Come on!" he groaned, more disappointed and mildly irritated than terrified. "My eye too, now?"

Worm realized he was in a chair somewhere other than Carcosa, or perhaps somewhere inside Carcosa, but in a different room than the one with the three Antiochians and the stripper and the chopped and screwed New Order soundtrack. This room seemed special. *Important.*

The amber glow of the gas lamps illuminated the room around Worm and cast shadows all over the rich mahogany walls. Scattered about were button-tufted wing backs with burgundy, leather upholstery. Chippendale pieces of rosewood and maple furniture lined the perimeter of the room. The carpet—a deep, rich, maroon color, like clotted blood. On top of a crown oak, veneer case with crossbanding and diamond relief sat a Waterford crystal decanter, a bottle of Ouzo next to it.

He knew all about this shit. Back when he was pulling B&E's in Roland Park, he could get this kind of antique furniture off easily.

Across from him was a crotch mahogany breakfront with Movingue banding. $60,000, easy.

Crystal decanters and carafes filled the shelves behind the individually paned glass doors, their star of Edinburgh faceting and Lochnagar swirling patterns radiating silver and white. Some of the glasses were $150 on the low end, each, the decanters much more. Worm knew less about good crystal than furniture.

Someone had brought Worm's axe inside and leaned it against the beautiful furniture. The bloody weapon had no business being so close to such rare work.

In the space between Worm and the mahogany display cabinet was a luxuriously upholstered guest chair with cabriole and ball-and-claw foot legs. $12,000 each.

He realized he was sitting in the same type of chair. It was actually not comfortable.

Worm had pulled burglary jobs but never any home

invasions. He would never do that. He was a piece of shit but not that much of one. *Right?* he wondered. *Am I?*

Breaking into houses on Keswick Road but nobody was home, nobody got hurt. They would pull up in a U-Haul rented in some random junky's name and load all the furniture into the truck. He had pulled a truck heist along Route 29 with some of the friends he no longer had, hijacking an eighteen-wheeler that was packed top to bottom with some kind of estate sale furniture situation. There were other things, more than furniture. Ancient jewelry, music boxes and things of that nature, things that he hadn't had time to research.

There used to be a fence in Belvedere Square. A guy who owned a furniture store that was similar to Restoration Hardware. High end product. The owner didn't ask any questions. It was strange to imagine him reselling the stolen furniture to the same demographic it had been looted from.

The space between his upper eyelid and eyebrow burned like dry ice. "I'm tired of getting fucked up and waking up in brand new places. This is like the fourth time that shit's happened today."

A massive man with eyes sunk deep under his forehead entered the room. "I am Arturo. You caused quite a commotion out front. Brought us a lot of unnecessary attention."

Worm tried to nod, instantly wishing he had not. It felt like someone was driving a knife through his sinuses. "My bad."

"You're calm because you are without an amygdala now."

"I figured."

"You *figured*?"

"I saw the video. Y'all were playing that shit for me before you did it. Like right before. The fuck, man."

"So then you have nothing to fear."

"Fear? I wasn't scared of y'all weirdos to begin with."

Arturo smirked. "I wouldn't have wasted the procedure on you. Normally, I would just feed you to the Antiochians and be done with you, but Obelix wants to meet you personally. He finds this all...*interesting*."

"What the fuck is an Obelix?" asked Worm.

Arturo slugged him in the gut. Worm doubled over and clutched his stomach. "Your disrespect is irrelevant. You will die here today. There is no doubt about it. And you will die without the privilege of being sculpted. Your body will be disposed of in a fashion that leaves doubt in the minds of your loved ones as to whether you are dead, or not dead. That is to say, your body will never be discovered. No one will ever hear the story of how you talked tough. No one will know how you died. It will save you so much pain."

Worm hugged his arms around his body. When he sat back up, his forearms were covered in blood. He wiped the back of his hand over his mouth, tasted wet nickels.

There was something uncanny, something wrong about the man called Arturo's face. Nothing you noticed at first glance. His monstrous build, his massive fists, the way clothing hung from his frame like event staging drapery—all of these things made his acromegalic features look *normal*. But the longer Worm studied the man behind a crimson filter of subconjunctival hemorrhages, the more convinced he was that nothing was normal about the man called Arturo.

"Yo. What's the story with these Antiochian motherfuckers?"

Arturo played with a pastel pink Tamagotchi. "They work for us, sometimes. They're from Antioch."

Worm watched the big man as he stared intensely at the tiny plastic egg. "Like in the Bible?"

"Perhaps. Or maybe Antioch as in the eastern parts of Florida next to Lake Thonotosassa. It's irrelevant."

"Oh, it's relevant," Worm said. "They're fucked up. They don't belong in Baltimore."

Arturo shrugged and went back to his Tamagotchi.

The door opened and the man from Worm's vision entered the room. "Hello there. My name is Obelix and all of this is mine."

Worm looked in the man's large, gray eyes, his thick eyelashes. He pulled at his restraints.

"Please, don't," said Obelix. "I am inexorable. You will only succeed in bruising your wrists. How do you feel now?"

"I feel like somebody just took my eye."

Obelix laughed. "This is true. But you must feel liberated. To live in fear is to never be free, no?"

Worm coughed up blood onto his white T.

"Do you know what this is?" The large man leaned in closer, his hair falling over his shoulders and hanging close enough for Worm to smell his shampoo. He held a metal object at eye level so Worm could see it.

Worm shook his head, wincing and immediately regretting it. "Use your words."

"No."

Obelix laughed. "*No*, you will not use your words as I have requested? Or, *no,* as in you do not know of this artifact?"

"*No,* as in I don't know what the fuck that thing is."

Obelix held out the metal contraption, about the size of a man's head. "This is the Rood of Grace. An automaton. The world believed it was destroyed over 500 years ago. This treasure, it was buried below Boxley Abbey, deep down below. In life, anything can be accomplished with the right price and a discreet subcontractor with ground penetrating radar."

Worm looked closer. It was a mechanized crucifix. The eyes of the robot-Jesus moved back and forth in their metal sockets. Metal teeth chattered. Robot-Jesus grinned.

"The faithful idolized this contraption. After the discovery of its internal mechanism, the reformers used the Rood as evidence of the Catholic church's corruption. These religious types are not fond of human ingenuity masquerading as miracle."

Obelix rapped Worm on the temple with the Rood until it drew blood.

"What the fuck?!" Worm cried out. The warm blood trickled down his forehead and into his eye.

The tall man placed the Rood on the bookshelf. He clasped his hands behind his back and paced. "But tell me! What is more miraculous than human ingenuity? In the old days, we would skin interlopers such as yourself with a fleshing knife. A full body flensing. How crude! How barbaric! The inconsistencies, the lack of symmetry. We still remove the skin, but we no longer use such a primitive process."

Worm's brain throbbed inside his skull as if it were trying to escape. The pain was intense. He could no longer feel the tips of his toes.

"Now we are much more elegant. Tasteful. We have perfected the process."

"My man," Worm groaned. "Can you please stop talking? I gotta be back before 9:00 p.m., not a minute passed or they put me back in the joint. I ain't trying to miss curfew, feel me? And you keep running your mouth about dumb shit."

Obelix laughed, then smacked Worm across the face and continued. "We have, how you say, *streamlined* the skin removal process. The interloper is strung up on the Pau de Arara. That is to say, a long, metal conduit is placed over the interloper's biceps and behind the knees, while the ankles and wrists are bound together. The man and the pole are suspended between two marble platforms. The interloper hangs upside down, his appearance much like a hibernating bat."

Worm sighed. "Why is it that the primary antagonist at the end of the story always wants to tell you about his master plan before he kills you? I don't give a fuck about none of that shit you talkin' about."

Obelix rotated the gold ring on his pinky so that the large ruby embedded in it faced outward. "The interloper hangs from the Pau de Arara and we put him on an IV of sulfamethoxazole and trimethoprim. This combination of antibiotics is administered in extreme amounts over a period of forty-eight hours. The result is toxic epidermal necrolysis. The skin falls off completely. Can you imagine? On its own. It truly does. It just falls away, perfectly, at the same speed and consistency. Like meat in a crockpot. The aesthetics are so pleasing. Nothing at all like the savage art of skinning a man with a fleshing tool. When the interloper's body is discovered by his countrymen, they see the precision. They see that great care was taken."

"Goddamn."

"Ah." Obelix waved his hand dismissively. "Not everyone is an artist. I do not expect someone such as yourself to appreciate the intrinsic value of art."

"You don't know what I've been through."

"And yet, I have known so many like you. The names and faces have blurred together over the years, as if you were all the same person. Perhaps you all are. Your only intrinsic value is the raw material your body provides. Until you have been transmogrified, you are nothing more than sculpting clay, waiting for the touch of a true artisan. I would love to show you this process. Let you experience this art form. Unfortunately, we do not have forty-eight hours. Or, I should say, *you* do not have forty-eight hours."

Arturo carried the mechanized Jesus out of the room.

"Why?" Worm asked.

"Why, what?"

"Why make this shit? Why mass produce it and flood the city with it?"

"I make it for the sake of art. Art is only true art when it cannot be replicated. Death is the only theater of art left uncharted. A death cannot be replicated. No two people are alike, so no two deaths can be either. This *shit,* as you say, is simply a catalyst. Through it, we can achieve divine art, the likes of which have never been seen before."

"For art."

Obelix sneered. "You say it as if there is anything more important."

"Why here? Why Baltimore?"

Obelix started to pace again. "Did you know that there were 343 killings in Baltimore last year? That amounts to fifty-eight murders for every 100,000 residents. Since 2014, the city's murder rate has increased by 65%. No one cares, no one notices. A few more drug dealers go missing. Perhaps the amount of junkies turning up in the city morgue increases. We are speaking about junkies and dope pushers, yes? These are not newsworthy occurrences. In Baltimore, an artist can stay under the radar without limiting his creative needs. Besides, I like it here."

Arturo came back in the room and closed the door behind him. He stood in front of the door, a mountain of a man with a nose that looked like a bruised gourd. "*Me sinhorís,* but we have prior engagements in thirty minutes and—"

"Tilapia," said Obelix, lifting up Worm's chin so he could look directly into his bloodied eye. "You know this fish, yes?"

Worm twisted his face away from the Greek and spit out a tooth.

"In my youth, I labored over catfish at a small fish farm in Kozani, near Lake Polyfytos. Every two runs we would raise a crop of tilapia instead of catfish. The reason for this? The tilapia would clean the ponds. This fish, you see, it will eat all of the leftover food and catfish shit, and in the process of doing so, it will clean the water, preparing the ponds for the next cycle of catfish. Do you understand my allegory? Do you understand the subtext?"

Worm had started to lose consciousness so Obelix woke him by jamming his fingers into his nostrils and pulling him upright. Something in Worm's nose cracked, then went soft. His eyes clicked open like a doll.

"Shall I continue? As I was saying, this fish, this tilapia, it is a fish that eats the leftover food and excrement of the catfish. Imagine, a bottom feeder so lowly, so disgusting that it will eat the waste of the catfish. You are the tilapia in this anecdote, yes? And yet, you come for me? You want to play big tuna in my ocean, *malaka*? *Sikothíkane t' angoúria na gamísoun to manávi*! You fuck. Who do you think you are?"

Worm sucked his teeth. "I hate this fucking city. Everything about it, I hate. I hate the poor white trash in Dundalk and Pigtown and Highlandtown with their packs of bastard children, each with different last names, all of them on medical assistance, their parents on methadone and suboxone. I hate the stupid, black, ignorant dope dealers with their Cartier frames and slick talk, their little brothers riding around on dirt bikes in the middle of Pratt Street while the old money liberals clutch their pearls, talking about how taxes need to be spent to build a dirt bike track for these bike kids, so out of touch, not knowing the reason the kids ride the bikes in the middle of the city in the first place. I hate the Squeegee Boys and club music. I hate you greasy Greek fucks with your blue and white flags and your Ouzo breath and your sweat smelling like *kontosouvli*. I hate the potholes and dilapidated tennis courts, basketball courts with the nets and hoops removed to *discourage* loitering. I hate the junkies and the clinics and the needle exchanges. I hate Johns Hopkins and how they buy everything up and then sit on it, letting it rot until they can demolish the whole block and turn the neighborhood into their newest medical building. And I hate fuckin Old Bay seasoning. I hate that shit with a passion. Everybody loves that shit but it's too salty to me. Same thing with Snow Balls. One time I did a bid out of state and I was talking about custard Snow Balls with extra marshmallow and my cell buddy told me that shit is not unique to Baltimore. That lots of places have them. That was tough for me to find out. But this is *my* city. I'm *from* here. I was born here. You don't get to fuck shit up for me. This isn't yours to fuck up. You have to coexist here or not exist."

The lack of fear was exhilarating.

Obelix burst into raucous laughter. "He is being serious, yes? Arturo please do not tell me that what we have here is a fucking superhero, come to save the world with his vigilante justice? This is what he means, yes? He wants to save the city? Our little tilapia wants to save his tiny, little pond?"

"I believe that is what he is saying," Arturo said.

Obelix smiled without showing his teeth. "Oh, this is rich."

Arturo snorted. "Indeed it is."

"And of this vigilante justice, *malaka*," asked Obelix, "what was your plan?"

Arturo put his finger to his earpiece. Something was happening on the loading bay side of the building. "Repeat that," he demanded.

"Something is coming at—." The voice in Arturo's earpiece cut off.

Worm felt the shockwave in his bones. It was like someone dropped a mic on stage at a concert.

"I got a gun that can lift up a car"
- YG Addie

20

"Was that a fucking bomb?" Obelix screamed over the roar of furniture shaking.

The vibrations settled and the sound of impossibly large footsteps came from somewhere nearby. The men all stared at each other, shocked by the violent disruption.

Obelix looked incredulously at Arturo. "Well go and find out then, man!"

Arturo ran into the room with his gun drawn.

It sounded as if bookcases were tumbling like dominos, punctuated by shrill metallic screeching. Obelix looked Worm up and down. "Don't move," he said, then ran into the other room.

There were more screeches of metal on metal, and then the sound of the high pressure shop air he had access to in the prison optical lab. He didn't wait long before following Obelix into the other room.

They stood in a laboratory of some kind; stainless steel equipment and large vats stretched to the ceiling and covered every surface. Powder blue liquid spun in a centrifuge. Tubing stretched from vat to vat, running down the sides of the metal and along the exposed walls. Actuators and servo valves dotted the walls like pimples. Worm watched the glowing fluid circulate through the tubing, how it ran loops of winding, neon blue barbed wire down the length of the armature.

Standing above it all was Sweet Breath. Ten feet tall and encased in a titanium exoskeleton, blades and sharp edges sticking out of the housing. Gatling guns or rocket launchers or both attached to the arm cages, ammunition swinging like rapper jewelry.

Mecha-Sweet Breath.

"What the fuck?" Worm wiped the blood from his eyes. "I killed this fat bitch already."

"Ha!" Sweet Breath swung his arm up and Worm dove into a somersault. The flechette rounds whizzed above his head, nearly taking his scalp off.

"Take cover, boss!" Arturo screamed. He had taken shelter behind a turned over table. "Take this, motherfucker!" Arturo fired at Mecha-Sweet Breath. The bullets bounced off the metal caging and ricocheted around the room.

"Deez nuts!" Sweet Breath swung out his other arm and fired the rocket launcher. An anti-tank missile seemed to float out of the launch tube in slow motion then slam into the steel vats behind Arturo. Sweet Breath fired another ordinance and a hole opened up in one of the vats. Worm hid behind the brushed steel.

Blue liquid sprayed out of the puncture hole in the vat and rained down over Arturo. "It burns! Oh God!" he screamed. The skin on his forehead began to bubble.

Blood ran down Sweet Breath's cheek and down his neck. "That boy got fucked up!"

Worm watched it all from behind the steel vat.

Arturo rubbed his eyes with his palms, then screamed as his eyelids and the skin of his forehead came off with his hands. The large man doubled over and made hissing noises as his back split open. Slick, gray tentacles sprung out of his shoulder blades like bungee cords and attached themselves to the ceiling.

"Oh hell naw!" Sweet Breath aimed the needlegun at the Arturo-thing and fired. The dart-shaped ammunition hit the Arturo-thing in the chest, tearing apart his flesh. More gray tentacles leaped out of the wounds and hovered in front of the Arturo-thing, twirling in the air like gymnastic ribbons. The tentacles moved in slow, flowing movements, spiraling in large circles while growing longer.

"What...is...happening...to...me?" The Arturo-thing had sprouted more tentacles; some as thick as PVC pipe and covered in glowing, green ichor. The skin on his face was gone and flashes of white bone, speckled with yellow globules of fat were visible under the exposed subcutaneous tissue. Worm could see the fear in his eyes.

Mecha-Sweet Breath aimed an arm-mounted MK-153 and let go another anti-tank rocket. Instantly, the thickest of the tentacles snapped out and wrapped themselves around the ordinance, strangling it to the ground before it could take out the Aturo-thing. There was a loud boom, deep and full of bass like an 808 that Worm felt in his solar plexus. He tried to swallow but the back of his throat was like sandpaper. The tentacles pulsed with the rocket, absorbing the kinetic energy of the explosion while the Arturo-thing screamed in pain.

"Oh fuck! Oh God help me!"

Two tentacles burst from below the Arturo-thing's waist; long phallic things that stretched out and penetrated Mecha-Sweet Breath in between the melting caging of the robotic exosuit. Veins ran around the long gray cables, throbbing as the mutations drilled deeper into his intercostal muscles. Blood bubbled in the corners of Mecha-Sweet Breath's mouth. He held his jaws tight together, his lips pursed and eyes squinting so that he resembled a disapproving elderly woman.

Suddenly, the tentacles retracted, taking most of Mecha-Sweet Breath's internal organs with them. Ropes of guts spread out onto the floor with a wet smack.

The Arturo-thing roared. The sound of his voice was different now, as if he had multiple sets of vocal chords. He turned his bloody head and then he was staring right at Worm.

"You know this shit ain't right."

For a moment Worm could see the Arturo-thing was still intelligent, the light behind his eyes vibrant and aware. The monster whimpered, then ran through the wall of the stash room, his tentacles tearing down the concrete and leaving destruction in his wake. Worm watched the creature that used to be a bodyguard, or some kind of second-incommand to a local gangster, loping off into the sunset while his tentacles unfurled and made flapping patterns like the spines of invisible wings.

A paisley pink Tamagotchi clattered to the floor. Worm picked it up and studied the LCD screen. A pixelated image of an egg blinked and then cracked open. Tentacles shot out of the egg and blinked on the toy's screen.

Worm threw the Tamogotchi at the wall and said, "Oh you bitch."

Orange light smacked him in the face through the Arturo-thing-sized hole in the wall. That meant curfew was coming. He heard another roar in the distance, followed by the sound of an explosion and a car alarm going off. The Arturo-thing was a problem Worm would have to deal with another time.

Flames had begun to dance in the corners of the room. A waste basket has turned over and a pile of papers burned underneath a drafting table.

"Wait!"

Worm turned around. It was Mecha-Sweet Breath or Sweet Breath or whatever he was now.

"Please. Just one thing."

"No."

"Just post me on your Instagram. Please."

The drug dealer with one foot looked like he was trying to smile then died before Worm could remind him that he didn't have an Instagram or a phone yet. Sweet Breath's veneers shined under the warehouse lights.

Worm found Obelix hiding behind the drug processing armature. "I see you're still alive."

The leader of the Greeks sat in a pool of blood, his back propped up against one of the steel vats. "For now, yes. And later as well. There is no providence. There is no teleological reason for any of this. God is just a substance. A substance to be used. All of this– "

The injured man was interrupted by a round of violent coughing. Blood ran over his lower lip.

'Oh ard," Worm said, squatting in front of Obelix. "All of this is yours. Or some other dumb shit that's supposed to sound tough. I'm already hip."

"God is not inside you. God is not inside you like God is in me. The substance flows through me. God is a part of me and I am a part of God. You are on the outside looking in. You have no great substance, no place in the universe."

"Yo." Worm shook his head and wiped blood out of the wound where his eye once was. "You talk and you talk. The only place I gotta be is that halfway house before curfew. I'll take it one day at a time."

"You will see." Obelix clutched his midsection, his black Oxford stained darker with wetness. Blood ran between his fingers and over his knuckles, crawling down his forearm in streaks of red.

"You got fucked up, " said Worm.

"Flesh wounds." Obelix waved a dismissive hand.

"You know I'm gonna kill you, yo. It's the whole reason I'm here."

Obelix looked up at Worm, searching his face. "What is your name?"

"Who cares? You about to be dead as fuck anyway."

"I care."

"Worm."

Obelix frowned. "*Skouliki*? This is a name?"

"Yeah motherfucker, *my* name. Shit."

"Well then, *Worm*," Obelix chuckled. "Our great Worm. Let his name be their battle cry."

Time had run out. He had listened to this man for long enough and it was time to end this. Worm grabbed Obelix and swung him by his hair and shirtfront. The leader of the Greeks sailed across the room and crashed into the crotch mahogany breakfront. Worm stood, transfixed by the destruction. The exploding glass looked like slivers of ice in the winter, the kind you find in potholes and can pull out in the form of big, manhole-sized sheets, trying to keep them solid for as long as possible, before they inevitably split into smaller pieces and are gone forever.

I could be gone forever, Worm thought, and then immediately knew that this was a fantasy and always would be. Nothing more. All he could do was try to make it back to the halfway house in time for curfew.

Obelix twitched on the floor. "Oh no. Not like this. This is not providence. This is *not* theatrical. This is not theatrical at all."

Worm was stronger. Without fear. He saw that his axe had fallen off the wall and landed near the tall man's feet. "This is over. The city has been through enough."

With one motion, he lifted the axe from the ground and over his shoulder, then swung it back down on Obelix's neck, putting all of his weight into it.

Hot blood peppered Worm's face. The crabcake from earlier did somersaults in his stomach, forcing him to suck in air between his teeth.

He looked down.

Obelix was still alive. The axe had only gone through a third of his neck. Worm had no choice but to lift up the axe and bring it down again.

And again.

Worm hacked until the room looked like something he had seen in juvenile detention. In a place called the Charles H. Hickey School for Boys, in the county somewhere unimportant. A kid, probably no more than 14 years old, got stuck in the laundry room by some other kid. Got poked in his stomach and thigh a bunch of times. The femoral artery. Worm had to clean out the laundry room afterwards. Blood had covered the tile walls in long brush strokes of burgundy. Some of the splatter marks were thin stringy-things like the delicate gossamer of a spider's web; some thicker and three dimensional like pieces of red spaghetti stuck to the wall. Others were ink blots and big, circular splotches.

Worm felt the warm droplets of blood on his face and wondered if he looked like the tile walls of the laundry room. When Obelix's head had been completely severed from his body, Worm dropped the axe and walked into the streets.

*"I don't give a fuck about no money or no bitches
and I aint even lying,
I don't care about the fame, I just wish I wasn't dying"*
- Smash

21

It must have been close to 9:00 p.m. The neon signage outside of Carcosa glowed red into the night. Bats replaced birds and moths replaced flies. Worm stepped onto Newkirk Street, holding Obelix's severed head by the hair. The head swayed back and forth, bouncing off of his hip as he walked. Behind him, Carcosa burned. He listened to what sounded like screams, but could have been the roar of flames, coming from inside.

Worm put out his hand and tried to wave a hack down. It wasn't hard to find one in the city. When no one stopped for him, he wondered if Obelix's head was the problem. He dropped it, then kicked it away, watching it roll off the curb and bounce into the street.

Maybe it was him. He was bloody, beat up. He had taken Obelix's tie and wrapped it around his head in an attempt at covering the empty eye socket but he knew it only made him look crazier, walking around Greektown with a bloodstained Hermes tied around his fucked up face.

Some time passed before a champagne Toyota Corolla, mid-2000's body style, pulled up to the curb.

The driver rolled the window down and leaned over the passenger seat. "Where you going?"

"Over Rose Hill," Worm replied. "Old York and Cator."

"Aite. Get in."

Worm got in the backseat and pressed his fingers into the upholstery. He still had that overwhelming desire to feel, to touch. Blood flowed freely from his empty eye socket.

"You aite, yo?" The hack looked at him through the rear view mirror.

"I'm good."

"I'm saying though, you look a little fucked up."

Worm pressed himself deeper into the seat and closed his eyes. "I'm better than ever. Everything is good now."

They came to a red light at East Monument Street and idled. "I don't know man. It looks like somebody shot you in the head or some shit."

"Yeah, man. Something like that."

The hack's eyes widened. "For real? Somebody shot you in the head?"

"Not exactly. It's cool, man. This is just another speed bump on my road to happiness."

The hack laughed. "My man! Speed bump on the road to happiness. I like that."

The light turned green and they made a right onto Edison. They rode in silence until they reached The Alameda.

"You trying to put on some music or something?" asked Worm.

"Sure." The hack reached back, holding out a purple auxiliary cord. "Plug your shit up, play whatever you want."

"Ain't got no phone."

"Who the fuck doesn't have a phone?"

Worm's skull pounded. "That would be me I guess."

The hack took the cord and plugged it into his own phone. "What you want to listen to?"

"Play something by Marvin. *Inner City Blues* works for me."

"Marvin!" The hack slapped his knee. "What you know about some Marvin?"

"Man, I know enough. Just play that joint."

"Ok bet, I got you, I got you. I'll pull it up on YouTube. One second."

The hack made a left on Argonne Drive and the piano keys and triangle chimes of the intro began to play through the Corolla's stock speakers. Marvin had played the piano on the original recording. Worm loved that piano. They continued down Argonne, making a slight left as the sound of Bobbye Jean Hall's iconic bongos began.

What now? he wondered. *What happens next?*

Bobby Babbitt dropped in with his funk-propelled bass line. A lonely saxophone seemed to sneak into the background and then retreat as fast as it had come. They rode while Marvin hit his falsetto and the Funk Brothers provided the backbeat percussion. The string section began to rise above the drums, gradually building tension, his vocals demanding urgency.

"Bro," Worm said. "I fucking hate it here."

"You geekin," said the hack. "Fuck you mean you hate it here?"

Worm sighed. "Nah, I mean, I love it, too. I just hate it too, you know?"

The hack laughed. "Do I."

They made it to Old York Road as the open octaves droned on, making everything bleak and hollow. The hack pulled to the curb. It was 8:54 p.m. Worm rummaged through his pockets and came out with the crumpled hundreds and twenties he had gotten from Sweet Breath.

"Say man." The hack had turned around. "We good."

Worm frowned. "What you mean?"

"What I said."

Worm still held out the bloodstained money.

"Put that away. We straight."

"Why?"

"I don't know. "

"My man." Worm got out the car and approached the halfway house.

He had made it somehow, and he had nothing to fear. The Arturo-thing would be a problem, something he would have to deal with but there was always tomorrow. He had made it back to the spot before curfew and nobody could tell him anything. He had time now.

Worm slumped against the door and knocked.

"Oh shit," an effeminate man's voice said from inside the rowhouse. "Somebody about to miss curfew. You had three minutes before this door was finna be locked on your goofy-ass."

Worm's vision began to darken at the edges. His head throbbed. The sound of deadbolts unlocking went down the length of the door. Worm knocked again.

"Do you not hear me opening this shit up, hon?"

He had his whole life ahead of him. He had made the city—therefore the world—a better place. Sure, he had only stopped one monster in a city full of supervillains, and yeah, the Antiochians were still an unknown quantity that had to be dealt with, but there was time now. Things could be better. He would be better. Maybe he wasn't a whole piece of shit.

It wasn't quite 9:00 p.m. when the last deadbolt clicked. Worm began to fall as the door opened, his peripheral vision shrinking until his visual field was nothing more than a pinprick.

What's next for me? he wondered. *Where do I go from here?* Worm made sure to put one arm through the door frame of the halfway house before he started falling.

ACKNOWLEDGMENTS

To Jada, for telling me to do this shit. Two years ago I shared something I wrote with you. It was a story about heroin and exotic cheese called The Wheel of San Geronimo. You told me to do something with it, to send that joint somewhere. I did, and they paid me for it, in real human money. I had never made money off something I wrote. Now I got this whole book and shit. None of this would have happened without you. None of it. I love you.

To my daughter, Juno, you're a baby, but I read this to you as I was writing it, and that really helped me figure it all out, to Mom and Dad, for putting me on to all those Stephen King and Dean Koontz books when I was coming up, my sister, for always having my back, Infa Redz for this TDH gangster shit, Jermaine Fontanelle for the detailed info about prison in Baltimore, my mother-in-law, Carolyn Ali for teaching me about Baltimore's past, Dr Joshua Broden for answering all of those late night questions about diabetes, rare diseases and medical instruments, Getum Verb, for introducing me to the Eastside of Baltimore, To J. David Osborne for all the guidance and direction, Kelby Losack for showing me that there are other people like me out there, writing about the people and places we write about, to A.A. Medina for the cover art, Brian Evenson for the support and encouragement, D. Harlan Wilson for always showing love, and to all the folks who offered wisdom or friendship along the way; Grant Wamack, Eddie Rathke, Bud Smith, Robert Vaughan, Antero Pietila, Craig Clevenger, Nadia Bulkin, Richard Rothstein, Jeremy Robert Johnson, Gabriella Decker, Smash, E. A. Petricone, Nathan Ballingrud, Matthew Stokoe, Edward Lee, Andre Duza, Ryu Murakami, Donald Goines, Dr. Samantha House, Tyree Colion, Tom Over, Iceberg Slim, D. C. Don Juan, Topp Dogg Hill, everyone who supported me on my journey and the city of Baltimore, Maryland.

ABOUT THE AUTHOR

David Simmons lives in Baltimore, MD with his wife and daughter.

Visit brokenriverbooks.com for our full catalogue.

Thank you for picking up this title.

Fucking good, right?

Made in the USA
Middletown, DE
24 February 2023